YOM KIPPUR

THE DAY OF ATONEMENT

Silvia Ruarte Funes

iUniverse, Inc.
Bloomington

YOM KIPPUR
THE DAY OF ATONEMENT

iUniverse books may be ordered through booksellers or by contacting:

iUniverse
1663 Liberty Drive
Bloomington, IN 47403
www.iuniverse.com
1-800-Authors (1-800-288-4677)

ISBN: 978-1-4697-6149-7 (sc)
ISBN: 978-1-4697-5979-1 (e)

Printed in the United States of America

iUniverse rev. date: 12/10/2012

First and foremost, I give thanks to God for inspiring me. I am also grateful to my husband and my children: Gabriela, Gustavo, Marcos, Meliza, Mauricio, and Ingrid for their encouragement, and to my grandchildren who bring me joy.

A special thanks to Horacio Zain for his support and help with research and to Miriam for her prayers and intercession.

Thank you to Nayda Ortiz and Jorge Flores for some suggestions, to Cathy Trentini for translating the work into English, and to all the people and friends who have stood with me, working with so much love and so many words of encouragement.

A very special thank you goes to my daughter, Gabriela, for her love and patience. Thank you for sharing in this dream, which has come true.

May the light of this story impact the minds and hearts of both those who were involved in this sad history and present-day readers to bring forgiveness and reconciliation to all.

TABLE OF CONTENTS

CHAPTER 1   "Cleansing Operation"........................... 1

CHAPTER 2   "Time of Atonement"............................ 7

CHAPTER 3   "Captives of Pain" 13

CHAPTER 4   "Auschwitz" (A Spark in the Darkness) 19

CHAPTER 5   "Path of Light" 29

CHAPTER 6   "Treasure of Terror" (United in Danger).......... 35

CHAPTER 7   "In the Belly of the Fish"....................... 43

CHAPTER 8   "Mission in South America" (A Window of Hope). 53

CHAPTER 9   "From Hatred to Love" (Calm in Paradise)........ 65

CHAPTER 10   "David" (Roots of Resentment) 77

CHAPTER 11   "The Curse of the Gold" 83

CHAPTER 12   "The Calm Before the Storm" 97

CHAPTER 13   "Mortal Vortex" 103

CHAPTER 14   "Yom Kippur" (The Sun of Righteousness)....... 111

EPILOGUE... 123

"Cleansing Operation"

"Neither much gold nor much wealth will ever be imperishable treasures for man."

DENSE ARTILLERY FIRE SHOOK THE *Stuka* plane that Coronel Hans Müller fruitlessly piloted, trying to evade the intense artillery fire of the enemy. The advancement of the Allied forces had intensified to the extent that simultaneous combats were being fought on all fronts. Hans had advanced and penetrated the length of the German battle lines. As the attack intensified, the possibility of Hans maintaining his flight position decreased dramatically. The tension was augmenting.

Suddenly an English plane approached the right side of the cockpit in straight flight. The enemy's surprising stratagem and accurate shots did not allow the young German officer enough time to avoid the series of shots that struck the tail rudder, detaching a part that then flew through the sky. Losing control, the plane began a hallucinatory plunge that impeded any maneuver by the badly injured pilot.

As the warm blood gushed out, Coronel Hans Müller's right arm began to go numb. The desperate attempts of the Coronel and his co-pilot had not been able to stabilize the machine when a new discharge of projectiles fully impacted them. The seconds were endless for Hans, whose companion had toppled over in his seat with his chest bathed in blood. He was dead.

A gesture of desperation and pain engulfed the pilot's face as the fall continued vertiginous and out of control. With one last superhuman effort, Hans managed to eject himself from the flaming plane, which continued its violent descent. From the air he watched his machine explode among some trees and instantaneously it struck him: that very plane had been the one he used in the conquest and destruction of Czechoslovakia. As his parachute bore him downward, he considered the uncertain destiny that awaited him until the intense pain of his feet crashing against the hard ground shook him from his ruminations.

Immediately, his sense of smell was taken aback by the nauseating stench of the place of his landing. When he managed to lift himself up, he discerned dark columns of smoke rising from grey barracks in the distance. He instantly recognized the place: It was a concentration camp.

Hiding himself between the trees, Hans slowly dragged himself towards the nearest building that silhouetted before his tired eyes. The cold was intense, and Hans was weary, the loss of blood further depleting his strength. The unbearable odor wounded his nose and turned his stomach, urging him to go in the opposite direction, but his sense of self-preservation forced him to continue toward the barracks.

He reached the barbed wire fence and observed the movements of the guards. He tried to call out but everything started to spin dizzily around him as an unknown darkness flooded before him, and he collapsed limply to the humid ground, which received his weakened body as he fell. The last thing he heard was the barking of dogs approaching.

When Hans woke up, he found himself in a strange room. Its white walls and the acrid smell of medicines indicated that he was in some type of infirmary. Slowly, his blinking eyes got used to the light streaming in through the narrow window. It must have been noon. He had no idea of how long he had been unconscious.

The sound of approaching steps roused his curiosity. A thin, almost completely bald doctor with small spectacles that appeared to play on his aquiline nose entered the room. The two long teeth protruding from the doctor's lips as he greeted Hans with a thin smile reminded him of a preposterous caricature. Hans returned the greeting, stating his name and rank. The doctor informed him of his state of health and projected recovery period, which would last about a week and a half, seeing as the wound in his arm was relatively deep and needed time to scar. Miraculously, no bones were broken, but the doctor prescribed absolute rest.

The forced immobility made the following days seem interminable for the young official. From time to time, he could hear the pained cries of men and women coming from a distance. Later, he discovered that these cries were caused by merciless experiments and surgical operations performed without anesthesia, which signified mortal torture for many.

Hans couldn't help being shaken by the pain and despair of these people, who were being coldly tortured to death. He had developed a specific career in aviation, which kept him distant from and ignorant of certain aspects of the realities of German occupation. As a soldier, he was well acquainted with the horrors of battle, but torturing helpless, unarmed civilians was unfathomable in his code of honor: wartime or not. Nevertheless, his country was at war and Hans was well aware that he was but one soldier among the multifaceted ranks. His duty was obedience to the orders of his superiors and not arousing doubt of their methods, which would have certainly condemned him as a traitor.

His recovery came sooner than expected. Just three days later, he was sitting on his bed, standing up and taking a few steps. One afternoon he stood looking through a small window in the room, absorbed in his own thoughts. He was used to the constant sounds of people coming and going outside his room, but the sound of his door opening snapped him out of his pensive state. He turned his head in curiosity and encountered the same smile that received him his first day.

The doctor entered the room and declared, "Well, I see that you feel much better today. You're standing!"

"Yes, I do feel much better. I just needed some rest," Hans answered. "I would like to walk a bit. Could you tell me how I can get my boots cleaned? They are very muddy."

The doctor paused and looked directly at Hans. "There is a Jewish boy in charge of those tasks. Would you mind him doing this job for you?"

3

Hans looked back at him for a moment before answering, "I don't see why not; it doesn't bother me if he cleans them. Where can I find him?"

"Just a few moments ago he was cleaning the room next to this one. Shall I send him to you?"

"No, thank you. I need to walk. I'll look for him myself."

"As you wish," the doctor nodded as he turned and left the room.

In the adjacent room, Hans found a young boy who had apparently just finished cleaning the floor. He noticed raw blisters on his small yet calloused hands as he wrung out his mop. The faded rags that hung on his thin shoulders were damp with blotches of blood and dirty water. The tall soldier entering the room startled the boy, who jolted backwards, as if trying to escape. The official approached him and said, "Boy! Come here!"

A look of panic showed in the boy's eyes as the threatening shadow closed in on him. He froze in silence for an instant, unable to answer. Hans took him by the arm, perceiving at once the boy's terror and the residue of the grotesque tasks imposed upon him earlier that day, and gently asked, "Are you deaf?"

Dread had suppressed any swift reply, although the boy understood the German language well. Coming out of his stupor, his stuttering response was barely audible, "No, sir."

"What is your name?"

"David," he stammered, eyes staring downward in fear.

"Are you the one who cleans shoes?" The man spoke to him calmly, putting David at ease.

"Yes. Yes, sir. Would you like me to clean yours?"

"Yes, come with me. I want them to shine."

On their way back to Hans' room, a distracted guard who was rushing past them knocked David to the floor. "Clumsy Jew! Watch where you are going," he griped.

Tears filled David's eyes as he picked himself off of the floor. Hans detected more patches of dry blood on the boy's thread-bare clothes and holes worn into the soles of his tattered shoes. He noted something else, too—something he couldn't quite decipher.

When they entered the room, Hans pointed to the muddy boots in the corner.

"They will be ready soon, sir," answered the boy, who had gained his composure and, lifting Hans' heavy boots into his frail lap, began the task.

While David silently scraped and scrubbed, both were absorbed in their thoughts. Hans examined the child. How old was he? He looked so weak and small! There was something about the child that gnawed at his mind, something familiar: something from...something from his past, perhaps?

At the same time, David was surprised by the friendly behavior of this hard-faced soldier who, in spite of his initial rough appearance, was quite young. David quickly polished the soldier's boots, which shined to perfection. Seeing that the night was approaching, David nervously gathered his things. When he was almost at the door, Hans stopped him, pulled an exquisite chocolate bar from his pocket and placed it in his hand. With a slight smile, the official told him, "I'll expect you tomorrow again. I have more work for you."

That night, in the silence of the dismal barracks, David kept thinking of the unexpected encounter with the German officer and his unusual kindness. Not one of the other soldiers David had performed special tasks for had ever shown any sign of appreciation—much less shared a smile and a chocolate. Even at his tender age, David had learned to be cautious, especially of the German officers, but this man seemed to be different somehow. For the time being, lying there in his cot, he continued to savor the chocolate's delectable flavor, a sensation that he had practically forgotten.

Meanwhile, in the sterile surroundings of his hospital room, Hans was plagued with thoughts of the young Jewish boy who cleaned his boots. What was it about him that he couldn't shake? His thin frame? His pitiful appearance? The suffering expressed in his eyes? Hans dozed off with David on his mind. The next morning he woke up to a soft knock on the door. Rolling himself out of bed, he quickly got dressed. Opening the door, he looked down at the small body of the boy he had met the day before.

"G-g-good m-m-morning, sir," David faltered, "You asked me to report to you again today?"

"Oh, yes," Hans replied, "come in."

Every day after that, David was ordered to present himself to the officer of aviation, which he did with something close to happiness. These new duties were pulling him out of the painful routine of spectating so much suffering. As he worked, the solitary soldier told him that his name was Hans and that his plane had been taken down and fallen right there, in that place. David listened with childish wonder to the soldier's amazing accounts of flying and parachuting.

As David prepared to leave, Hans once again reached into his pocket and the boy relished the most delicious chocolate of his entire life. At first, David locked himself in air-tight silence in a suspicious fear of Hans. However, as the days went on, the cordial treatment Hans offered led him to converse as well.

One day, Hans surprised David by asking, "How did you get here? Where is your family?"

Those questions stirred scenes of the past in the child's mind: vivid memories of all that he had experienced in the past few years. For the first time, initially reluctant, David opened up to tell this stranger the incredibly story of his past.

"I remember it as if it had happened today:" he began, "our traditions, our celebrations, and especially those last moments I shared with my family in Warsaw. The war had begun...." David started to narrate as his soft, almost inaudible voice revealed, little by little, the pain he had held in his heart for so long.

Hans, in respectful silence, listened to his tale. He was absorbed in David, who between sobs, continued to relate his story. During those moments of conversation both escaped that loathsome place, being whisked back in time.

CHAPTER 2

"Time of Atonement"

"To ask for forgiveness, and to forgive, is not cowardice; rather, it marks the beginning of healing our own wounds."

"IT WAS 1940; WAR HAD broken out in Europe." David's story unfolded, his face growing somber with the memories.

"Several Jewish families still remained in hiding in Warsaw. My father, Gabriel Asser; my mother, Ruth; my sister, Sarah; my brother, Elijah; and I remained in the city. We did not know how long we could survive in those conditions...." The poignant innocence of the child's words transported Hans with him to his past.

Nazi soldiers patrolled the streets, searching for homes where Jewish families, who were often denounced by their Polish neighbors, were hiding. That afternoon Gabriel raced with his children, Sarah and David, to close the antique shop he owned. Upon arriving, he sadly looked around the place where he had worked for so long. Being surrounded by such fine works of art made him so happy. He briefly scanned the antique showcase that exhibited the beauty of ivory statues and various objects of silver and gold. Among them, a golden menorah stood out with its seven shining arms that reflected suddenly his eyes, which had filled with tears upon seeing it.

The rhythmic bells of the ancient clock hanging in the right corner of the shop announced that it was 4:30 in the afternoon. He instinctively lifted his gaze, being reminded that he would have to close quickly because there was a lot of movement in the streets that day and it wouldn't be easy to cross the city with so many soldiers everywhere.

Sarah, who always had helped him in the shop, was also in silent contemplation of that dear place. She broke the silence to remind him that they had to hurry because her mother was waiting for them to begin a special celebration; the most sacred day for Jews was about to begin: YOM KIPPUR, the Day of Atonement.

"Tell me more about this ceremony that is so sacred to you," Hans interrupted.

David, surprised by his interest, smiled slightly and began to explain why this celebration was so important to his people. "Yes, of course. Yom Kippur is the most solemn and sacred day of the year. It's a day when we make up with the Most High, our neighbor, and ourselves. We talk with the Eternal One, pray, confess our mistakes and ask for forgiveness. We can't get distracted; we must fast and pray all day," David explained.

"I see," Hans commented. "So, it really is an important day for you."

"In our Hebrew calendar, Yom Kippur begins at sunset on the ninth day of the month of *Tishri*, and we fast until sunset the following day. Yom Kippur is the Jewish day of repentance, and is the most important day of the year. We receive forgiveness from the Eternal One and reconciliation—my father taught me that word. It means we can be friends again because Hashem, our Eternal God, cleanses our hearts," continued David. "With our hearts all clean, we can also to ask for forgiveness and make up with anyone else we may have hurt or offended, even if we didn't mean to, according to Mosaic Law. Adonai grants us a new year that is happy and good when we are sorry for our sins. We all hope for this to happen this year, too."

Hans restlessly asked him, "What happened that afternoon when you left the shop?"

"Oh yes. I remember that evening like it happened yesterday...."

They hurriedly arrived home and quickly met around the table, which Ruth had lovingly set. The ceremony had to begin immediately. Gabriel placed the beautiful, golden Menorah he had brought from the shop upon the table. He had engraved all the names of his family members on its base, because he had chosen it as the Menorah that would replace the one that his father had inherited from his parents.

In deep emotion, tears ran down their cheeks as they considered their current situation, not knowing how much longer they would be together, or alive.

Ruth lit the candles on the Menorah in preparation for the meal, after which they would fast for a day. Gabriel's voice rose calmly and ceremoniously, beginning with the Kol Nidre prayer, imploring forgiveness. A deep silence full of peaceful vibrations accompanied his rhythmic invocation.

"And then what happened?" Hans interjected.

David's face grew gloomier as images flashed before him. Between the tears that blurred his eyes, those scenes that had repeated themselves so many times in his mind once again played before him. He saw himself worshipping the Eternal One with his family, united in one voice, intoning a sweet song that spoke of forgiveness.

Suddenly, the thunder of loud knocks at the door startled them. The door leading to the living room flung open and German soldiers stormed into the house. Terrified, they scrambled to find refuge further inside the house as the children dashed to seek the protection of their parents. The head soldier ran ahead of them and pitilessly struck their father across the face, knocking him back into his chair. With an anguished cry, their mother rushed to him, wiping the stream of blood that flowed from the corner of his mouth. The children observed the scene, paralyzed by fear. Each movement of those men, whose reasoning for all of this was incomprehensible to them, was etched in slow motion upon their hearts and minds.

Their nightmare had begun. The entire family was thrown into the back of a smelly truck and transported to what would become their lodging for the next two years: the Warsaw Ghetto. The most merciless extermination campaign ever carried out in history had begun against the Jews, and they had not yet begun to understand the magnitude of the cruelty and sadism exerted by Nazis.

The ghetto was surrounded by barbed wire, and thousands of Jews were massed together there without sufficient water. For several years they didn't have water to bathe in or comfortable beds to sleep on. At four o'clock each morning, they were led out, barefoot and in rags, to begin a day of forced labor. Their bodies were covered in sores and invaded by lice and other parasites. As time went on, a tremendous sensation of abandonment and desolation overwhelmed them. The only comfort that the family still clung to was the fact that they were still alive and together.

Elijah, the eldest brother, had discovered a way of avoiding the soldier's vigilance at the changing of the guards and often escaped to nearby farms for food. His escapades exposed the rest of the family to danger and caused a great deal anxiety for the fear he would be caught. During one of his raids, he was surprised by two soldiers, who beat him, leaving him unconscious and wounded. A farmer found him and, thinking him dead, returned him to the ghetto.

When Ruth saw her son, she threw herself on him and discovered that his heart was still beating. Alerted by her cries, the soldiers brutally dragged him away from her and, in front of the entire family, shot him squarely in the head, extinguishing any hope that he might have survived.

Days of anguish and pain followed the loss of Elijah. Nothing could lessen the desperation that was forming in their faces; their bodies deteriorated day by day in the endless agony. Their flesh disappeared and their skin started sticking to their bones turning them into walking skeletons.

The weak, the aged, and the dying were marched out daily toward common graves where they were forced to undress and remove their eyeglasses, dentures, and valuables, leaving no way of identifying their bodies once, at the edge of the mass grave, they were machine-gunned and plowed into the pit.

The soldiers would return with their horrendous booty to a special "collections" storeroom in the barracks, where they classified everything by placing the objects in different piles: clothes, shoes, jewels, spectacles, dentures. A Gestapo officer was in charge of all objects of value: gold, silver, or precious stones.

One day, Sarah recognized a doctor's daughter who was a friend of hers among those arriving. Her long, golden hair fell below her waist and had been the envy of her peers. That morning in the ghetto's central square, the German officer who separated the sick who would be executed from the strong who were able to work with a simple movement of his head pulled the girl out of the line. With a vicious smile, he cruelly fingered her hair and jeered, "What is this beauty visiting us today? What a pretty golden rug could be made out of this!"

The young girl shuttered and began to cry. With a sudden movement, the officer unleashed his gloved hand upon the young girl's face, drawing blood to her mouth before yelling, "Bring a barber! Quick!"

"No, no, please!" she pleaded.

"Please, you ask? You Jewish pig! On your knees! Say please again. I didn't hear you the first time!"

"For the love of God, don't hurt me!"

Losing control, the officer shouted in her face, "Shut up, you nasty pig; I want to make a rug out of your filthy hair!"

The barber was already on the spot, a razor in his hand. With a blow that knocked her senseless, the girl was dropped onto a chair and her golden hair brutally hacked off right in front of everyone. Sarah cried in distress as those golden locks fell to the ground while her friend's head was brutally shaved, as she relived the moment when her own red curls scattered across the dirty floor to the taunting of the soldiers that took her into custody and the shattering sobs of her mother.

They had witnessed similar scenes many times, having lost count of all time in the ghetto. Hundreds of people were executed daily. Their constant, silent prayer was for YHWH to give them strength to continue working and not be killed until they could leave that hell! And every night, in the silent gloom of the place where they slept, they gave thanks to the Eternal One for keeping them alive one more day, knowing that the following ones also were in his hands of love.

CHAPTER 3

"Captives of Pain"

"Do not remain captive in your limitations and despair.
God, with his love, has provided an escape for you."

HANS STARTED AT THE CHILD, dumbfounded by the candid
retelling that took him beyond the child's simple words to
revealing the bleak realities of German occupation. David's story
continued....

Several months later a new destiny awaited them. One morning after
they had lined up and were waiting to be marched off to their forced labor,
they were informed that they were being transferred to Auschwitz, a large
concentration camp actually composed of four smaller ones.

They were herded into trucks and taken to the railway station. There
the soldiers pushed them into closed cattle cars with no windows, just a side
opening through which the prisoners entered. They were forced to squeeze
in until they could barely move or breathe.

Once the cars were filled with what the soldiers deemed "human goods"
or "animals", they shoved the doors shut as they continued to heap insults
on them. Behind closed doors, they traveled for days in a horrible blackness
filled with groans and whimpers. Many died on the way. In their desperation
to feel some air, some stuck their toes through the spaces between the wooden
slats that made up the floor. They had no idea how long they had been
confined there, but their bodies had gone numb from the grueling trip.

Just when it appeared that strength had completely abandoned
them, the train came to a shrilling, abrupt stop. The side door jerked

open, revealing striking rays of sunlight that pierced their sight, which was weakened from their lengthy sentence as passengers caged in darkness. Their deadened bodies stumbled onto the platform, and as their eyes adjusted to the harsh light, they saw one another's wasted, ashen faces. Even the children had completely lost all luster of life from their eyes as every last trace of energy was being depleted.

Shading their stinging eyes with weak hands, they saw two rows of gray barracks divided by a wide lane leading to the entrance. In the background a large building that looked like a warehouse had a very tall chimney rising from its center. Black smoke snaked out of it now and then, and being dispersed by the cold wind, spread to each corner of the camp. Immediately, an assaulting stench penetrated their nostrils. It would take days for them to figure out what the strong odor from that disagreeable place was. Only time could lessen the repulsive impression it made.

Impacted by the suffering of the child and struck by this reality that had been unknown to him, Hans had avoided interrupting David's account. He had been so distanced from the inhumane treatment that the prisoners suffered. However, curiosity got the best of him, and he asked again, "Is your entire family here? Were you able to stay together?"

"No," David answered as he sadly gazed at the soldier and continued his time-altering story. "On that very horrible day we arrived, the soldiers began screaming their orders…"

The soldiers' punitive shouts tried to hurry the prisoners, but their cramped legs could not respond no matter how hard they tried to accelerate to avoid punishment. Several were brutally shoved and beaten, falling to the frozen ground without remedy.

One of their commands was for men and women to separate into two different lines. Ruth and Sarah did not want to leave the men in their family, but the soldiers' violent blows practically ripped them from their arms.

An anguished sob escaped David's lips as he re-lived that terrible moment, and with a stammering voice he went on, "Even now, I can see that long line of skinny, smelly, ragged women, with their shaven heads. As I watched them march away, I remembered my mother's beautiful face and my sister's smile. Not so long ago, I am sure all of those women were pretty, with long hair and nice clothes."

David explained that his last image of his mother, Ruth, was of a weakened, suffering woman who staggered when she walked and whose once lustrous face was bathed in tears. She tripped and tried to grab onto one of the women in front of her. With a tremendous crack, a soldier knocked her down face-first on the frozen ground. A deafening screech shook everyone.

"*Get up, you filthy, stinking Jew!*" *a soldier barked, kicking her straight in her kidneys with the tip of his boot. She fell and was unable to get back up, but the soldier insisted,* "*Get up! Obey me at once, curse you!*"

Just then, the line of men began to slowly move away. The figures of the women blurred in the tears that flooded their eyes. A fierce pain invaded David's chest; his heart had broken into pieces.

Their nightmare continued, but after a few days, David discovered that he could reach the distant barracks where his mother and sister were. Seeing Sarah was the highlight of his days, even though the stories they shared were unpleasant.

On one of those encounters, Sarah told David how on that dreadful afternoon of their arrival, she and the other women gathered Ruth's unconscious body and carried her into the barrack. Weeping uncontrollably, she fell on her knees beside mother, trying to wake her up. In her desperation, she began to cry in a voice that was little more than an anguished murmur. "*Oh Elohim, help us! Take us out of here!*"

Her repeated plea seemed to revive her mother's spirit, and she slowly moved her hand and began to caress Sarah's head as tears ran down her withered cheeks. In so short a time in the concentration camp, Ruth looked twice her age. Sarah held her close, only one question escaping her lips: "*Why?*"

Her answer was a long silence finally broken by the metallic noise of a switch turning off the light and a soldier's voice ordering them to go to sleep. But sleep was impossible. The afternoon that had separated the family scarred their minds.

David's fleeting moment of gladness was when he was able to meet his sister at the fence that separated them. They would talk for a few minutes, and she would tell him how she and mother were faring in that horrendous place. She said that the days went by slowly and the most tiring torture was the uncertainty of what would happen each day. She told him that very early in each morning, they were awakened by the violent slam of the door opening and the shouts of the guards that took them to work. Their mother worked, too, because she had recovered some of her vitality as the Eternal One renewed her strength.

Soon, due to her knowledge of art and antiques, Sarah was put to work in the camp's administration center, sorting the different objects of value stolen from the victims. Their visits were less frequent then, but one of the few times that they met, she quickly told him about the hundreds of different objects that passed through her hands each day: gold dentures, jewelry, eye glasses—literally, tons of articles made of gold.

Sarah was distraught thinking that some of those items are sold to pay for weapons that would be used to kill her people and to fabricate more bombs. She had heard some of the guards talking about new ones called V1 and V2. She had also heard them talking about some gas, cyclone B. She wasn't sure it was used for, but she could not ask more about it because had to be very careful that the guards who supervised her and the other workers did not find out she understood what they were saying.

Sarah also excitedly told David about a small book of art that she had found in a suitcase, all rolled up like an old parchment. The canvas was an oil painting with bright colors, but it wasn't the painting that really attracted her attention. It was the art catalogue that showed the beautiful, famous paintings and sculptures and whose French title brought to mind the marvelous moments that she had spent with their father in the antique shop, which seemed so far away now. Tears filled her tired eyes when she remembered how tenderly her father taught her all he knew about art, so when the guards weren't looking, she hid it in her clothes.

"Every spare moment that I have it in my hands is a delight. It makes me imagine myself strolling through a beautiful museum in Paris. It is my escape; it distracts my mind and distances me from the horrible reality that surrounds us," Sarah solemnly confided.

Sarah then told David of a new hope that had filtered into the camp. Rumors that Allied advances were piercing and weakening the German battlefronts reached the prisoners. As if to counteract these rumors, a new building was quickly assembled in a corner of the camp, sinister and mysterious.

Although her job sorting out dentures and other belongings at first disgusted her, Sarah would softly repeat a song to herself until it became part of her and she was able to forget her surroundings. How it encouraged

David to hear her proclaim in faith, "Believe me! We are going to get out of here! When you are sad, sing! Repeat your prayers quietly to yourself, 'Hevenu shalom aleicem.'"

Hans, cocked his head with curiosity, interrupting again to ask, "What does the song mean?"

With a soft voice David sang, "We bring you peace; peace be with you, always peace."

David paused a moment before continuing, "Sarah told me it would bring me peace that would let me endure anything, no matter what is happening around me. Now I sing it to myself all the time! When we said good-bye that day, we felt that even though we were prisoners being treated so unfairly, we could still feel the peace that the Eternal One gives to our hearts."

David's countenance soon darkened again....

His last conversation with his beloved Sarah was brief and painful. She had gone to find him at the barbed wire fence that separated them. Her face looked pale and her eyes had lost the glimmer of light he had seen in them at the previous encounter.

She seemed to be in a hurry, as if she wanted to break the news quickly so as not to cause more pain than necessary. She spoke with an anguished voice, "The woman's barracks are overflowing. A lot of new prisoners have arrived. There is no more room! Two days ago, when we lined up as usual, instead of marching us to work, a tall commander paraded through the endless rows of women, marking each step with that rhythmic clicking of his heals that sounds like a death march. I felt a chill go up my spine: a new danger was threating mother and me.

"He carried a rod which he indifferently used to touch the shoulders of many women, who began to tremble. He indicated that those selected should step out and form another line. Terrified, I watched as he tapped mother's shoulder! It all happened so fast that I was still in a state of stupor when I heard the commander's new order: 'Go on now, you rotten pigs! Today your filthy bodies will get a bath!'"

He ordered them to walk to the new, enclosed building. Not knowing what destiny awaited her mother, a sensation of uneasiness and pain penetrated Sarah's heart like a dagger. Ruth turned her face towards her daughter several times, capturing her with the desperation of her sweet gaze. It was as if she were hugging hug, embracing her with infinite tenderness.

"No! Not mother!" David's smothering cry shook Sarah, who cried uncontrollably as well. Their fingers clenched together even though the barbed wire separating them cut at their skin. They were unaware of that pain because the terrible anguish and the torment of never seeing their mother again were infinitely stronger. They would never again feel her arms of love and her sweet, comforting caresses.

Through the tears, Sarah continued, "When the doors shut, the rest of the prisoners were driven away to the labor site. I had the secret hope of seeing mother alive again, but the long night of waiting only deepened my conviction that I would never kiss her beloved face again."

Stifling a sob, she went on, "The next morning while I was working, I was horrified when mother Ruth's belongings passed through my hands to be classified. I had to force myself to not scream! Practically paralyzed by the pain, I continued working like a robot in the miserable classification of this cursed treasure that has cost the life of so many innocent victims!" Her voice faded, snuffed out by her sobs.

When they said good-bye that afternoon, they both noticed that their hands had smeared with blood; their blood had blended without their realizing it and bound them together, just as their shared pain for the loss of mother had. They both cried, promising one another to struggle to get out of that place and to reunite once again. This unbreakable covenant united them more than ever.

Sarah's final words surprised David. "Fight! Don't give up! I've been thinking a lot lately. I can still see, especially now that I am here with you, that mother's final glance was not just a tender, loving embrace for me. It was for all of us: for you, for father. But it was above all a sweet and tender farewell message saying, 'I love you! Keep fighting! You will be free!'"

David concluded his story saying, "A few months later, because of her knowledge and training, Sarah was transferred to another city as an art expert, and I haven't heard from her since. But I believe that we will see each other again because we are joined by strength, faith and mother's final message that tells us not to give up!"

CHAPTER 4

"Auschwitz"
(A Spark in the Darkness)

"The light of the just shines even in the dark, but the evil-minded will always walk in darkness."

THE DAYS THAT PREVIOUSLY WERE endless for David now seemed shorter. He was spending more time with Hans, who requested his presence often to ask him to do tasks for him as a pretext to talk with him more. David's story captivated him. He became acquainted with the young boy's family through his emotional narratives, which inadvertently touched his hardened heart. His brother's tragic fate, his sister's destitution, his mother's death, and David's tears had moved him. But today he had a new question for David, one that he asked directly, as soon as they began talking when he came to clean his room.

"Tell me, what has happened to your father? Is he still with you?"

"Let me start from the beginning. When we got here, we were assigned to one of the men's barracks. It was so crowded and smelly! The odor from the sweaty, unwashed bodies made me sick, and it took me a long time to get used to it because it was so strong. My job was to clean the torture and experiment rooms. I almost fainted when I arrived…"

As David approached the gray door with a cloudy glass window, he was greeted by the disgusting stench of blood mixed with excrement. When he opened the door, the smell provoked such nausea that he had to clean up his own vomit before proceeding to the deplorable task of preparing the room for the next "patient".

At night, his ears echoed with the cries and moans of the tortured prisoners, making it impossible for him to slumber. One night in particular, he closed his eyes tightly and turned on his side, trying to rest. His father, Gabriel, lay on the hard cot next to him. Still unable to sleep, he opened his eyes again and studied his father. He had aged some twenty years in their relatively short captivity. His cheeks were sunken and his dull eyes, clouded by the physical and spiritual fatigue that had burdened his soul, fell deep into their sockets. Feeling his son's gaze, Gabriel looked towards him. They had learned to express their thoughts and feelings by just looking at each other. That night, once again, they exchanged a well-known look that always came without words: How long will we last?

Even more insistently, David's eyes questioned his father, How is it that we are still alive?

As if he had expressed those thoughts out loud, Gabriel murmured, "I don't know, son. I don't know."

The prisoners in the barracks were dirty, worn out, and desperate. All but one, that is. On David's right, a small, peaceful man everybody called 'the Shepherd' had his cot. He spent his hours of rest immersed in a continuous prayer, mingled with strange songs that fascinated David even though he didn't understand them. They conveyed such peace.

David had spoken often with this peculiar person, who somehow seemed able to keep himself apart from this awful place. He had a different look in his eyes—they shone with a special brilliance. His words were never violent, but gentle and kind. It was as if he were already free! That night David felt a special sense of protection and safeguard in that place of pain and uncertainty as he lay between his father and the Shepherd.

The next day, for no particular reason, David felt gloomier than usual, thinking about my mother and sister. That night, he had a dream that his mother was calling to him, and he woke up weeping. His father was sleeping, exhausted from the day's work, and didn't hear him. But the Shepherd woke up and drew him near, comforting him with a warm embrace. The encouraging words he whispered into David's ear were forever engraved in his heart: "Even in this place, you are free. If the Son sets you free you, you are free indeed!"

Those words gave David a sense of great relief and hope. The Shepherd, speaking in a low voice so as not to awaken the other men, told him of someone who would come to be as the liberator. Every night after that, David fell asleep wondering what that liberator would look like and why it was taking him so long to come."

Hans stiffened, speechless. All at once, when David referred to his dream, Hans remembered: the night-waking, the floods of tears, the warm comfort of his own sweet mother. David reminded him of his own little brother! Sweet, innocent Adel! A terminal disease had taken his brother captive when he was just a child, much like this camp had imprisoned his innocuous friend.

Blinking back the burning tears that wanted to take over his eyes, Hans inquired, "Where is the Shepherd now?"

David somberly shook his head.

As time went on, the boy started to find peace in the midst of all of this suffering. Then one morning, a ray of sunlight coming through the opening that served as a window woke him up. It was later than usual. For some strange reason, the guards had not yet appeared to march them off to their allotted tasks.

Suddenly, a ruckus near entrance alerted the prisoners that the soldiers and their commanding officer were entering the barracks. They appeared with shouts and blows. David sensed that something terrible was about to happen. The soldiers commanded the prisoners to line up, and the commanding officer walked up and down the formation, his threatening eyes shooting flames as he gesticulated and yelled.

A prisoner had escaped that dawn, and the soldiers, after a cruel chase, found him and drug his lifeless body into the barracks, dumping the corpse onto the floor in front of everyone.

Enraged, the commander continued his horrid march. Fear provoked a deep silence that gripped at the captives' throats. Panic invaded the boy's mind. The inexorable death penalty would be applied in a different way this time. The commander's threatening finger pointed to the victims as the chilling death sentences gushed out of his mouth, "Get out of here, bastard!"

"The long, gloved fist struck random, terrified prisoners as he bellowed and pointed at the lifeless prisoner, "Look at that disgusting trash! That Jewish dung! Now you all will pay for his foolishness! No one gets out of here alive! May this be a lesson to all of you! Anyone else dare try?"

Silence was the only response he received.

"From now on, your work load will increase, and ten of you will pay the foolishness of this one! Ten of you will starve in the tank! There will be no food, no water! Only the cadavers of your grimy bodies will remain!"

Abruptly, his hand hit Gabriel's chest. David's heart stopped for an instant and he desperately clung to his father's waist, crying uncontrollably and pleading, "No, Father! Not you! You can't die!"

The calm, firm voice of the Shepherd broke the tension of the moment.

"Let him go, please. Please. I offer my life for his."

The furious face of the commander turned in astonishment toward him. No prisoner had ever had the nerve to speak up to him!

"Why, how dare you? Who do you think you are?" The commander stood eye-to-eye with the Shepherd, searing him with his stare.

"I'm just another prisoner, but let me take his place. He has a son, and I have no one."

After a few tense moments of silent expectation, to everyone's surprise, the commander uttered in an unobtrusive voice, "Very well," then quietly sneered, "Call out to your God to see if he can save you!"

David released his father and ran in aching desperation towards his friend, his companion of captivity, who had so often been a comfort to him. He held to him tightly, wanting him to stay. The Shepherd whispered for the last time in David's ear with his calm, sweet voice, "Have faith! Believe in the Son of the Eternal One. He will take you out of here."

With a stifling blow, the soldiers knocked David away from his friend.

"Noooooo!!!" The heartbreaking cry escaped David's throat, bouncing off of the walls and amplifying his voice as the soldiers led the ten victims away. Before disappearing out of sight, the Shepherd glanced towards him several times. With his last gesture, he lifted his eyes toward the sky and moved his lips, forming imperceptible words David knew were a final message of hope and courage. In spite of his suffering, a deep peace entered his soul as the thin silhouette of the prisoner blurred among his tears.

The prisoners taken to punishment as an example died in agony after many days in "the hunger cell", or as it was also known, "the death tank": no food, no water. Their pitiful groans were heard for several days until only silence surrounded the chamber that was the last earthly dwelling of the martyr. Still, David trusted that the Shepherd was resting in peace and that the Most High had given him his desired liberty."

"So, now only your father is with you?" Hans repeated his original question.

"Well, life went on without the Shepherd, but one afternoon, I saw several men talking in a corner of the barracks. Some prisoners were being moved to a factory to make weapons, and one of the men chosen to leave was my father…"

David spent that night in his father's arms. Together they recalled their life with mother, Sarah and Elijah. They remembered what a happy family they were. Then and there, they swore to each other that they would whatever it took to survive, and to be reunited again someday. That promise kept David alive; it kept him from falling into discouragement, and it would carry him to the end of the war when he would once again embrace his father and beloved sister, Sarah.

At daybreak David watched with red, swollen eyes as the soldiers entered the barracks to take the men away. He clung to his father's arm, and both cried desperately. A series of long nightmares from which David frantically wished to awake had begun. The soldiers struck him repeatedly to loosen his grip on his father, until he fainted, exhausted from the blows and sleepless night, and was taken to his cot.

The hours and days that followed changed David. He had become silent, not talking to his fellow prisoners and preferring to be alone. The only thing that kept him going was that flame of hope that burned in his heart—the promise he made to his father and the expectation of the arrival of the liberator that the Shepherd told him about so often.

He often wondered why he was still alive. He lived under constant beatings and the insults of the soldiers. His daily tasks varied, but usually he polished soldiers' boots, carried water, and mopped up the vomit, excrements and blood in the torture cells. Often, when he approached the infirmary ward, he heard the screams of torment coming from the patients used for experiments. A tall, thin doctor called 'the Angel of Death' was especially feared. The smell of death was everywhere! Just being alive in this place was a daily miracle!

When David finished his story, he exhaled a deep sigh. He felt as if a great part of his pain, so deeply hidden inside, had been released. He was relieved, although he also wondered uneasily what this German soldier would think of his story. Would he believe it or would he reject it? How much longer would he and Hans speak? Would Hans really turn out to be his friend?

Both were silent, deep in thought. The call of the guards alerted David that it was time to return to the barracks to rest.

"Hurry along. It will be dark soon, and I don't want you getting punished for being out so late," Hans murmured, showing concern for him.

As David dashed away, Hans inwardly admitted that without realizing it, he had started to grow fond of the boy. He understood the child's need for the care and protection of his father in this unbearable world of pain and death around them. Hans had already seen so much suffering: women lost their lives and even babies were mutilated. Death had become common to all, blind to age and condition. He began to worry about what would happen to his little Jewish friend who polished his boots.

Days after Hans' secret revelation, the camp's commanding officer called Hans to his office to discuss an important matter. He had received special orders from Berlin for the Luftwaffe official. The meeting occurred behind closed doors and without witnesses. Hans received orders to transport the gold that had accumulated from all the concentration camps: Auschwitz and its surrounding cities. As Hans left the commander's office, he acknowledged that although the task would be difficult to carry out, at least he could finally leave this unbearable place.

He had to develop a plan to mobilize the valuables in the shortest time possible to evade enemy attacks and confiscation. That night, he considered how he could remove the gold and other valuables, sending it to different parts of the world for safekeeping. He would transport it to countries in Europe like Liechtenstein and Switzerland, to far-off places like Tangier and Beirut, and even across the ocean to South America. He would have to smuggle the works of art along with the large amount of the gold that had already been turned into bars, branded with the eagle mark of the Reich and the SS. Most of the treasure: gold, precious stones, and different currencies of paper money would be taken by train to the SS headquarters in Berlin.

Although his task was simply to obey orders, Hans couldn't avoid thinking about the cost of the plunder in human lives. Its material value could be calculated to reach several billion dollars, but its value in suffering and misery was impossible to assess.

Although he was immersed in his plans, Hans' thoughts often turned to David. He knew the following day would be very busy, but wasn't able to close his eyes all night. An idea was blossoming in his mind that made his face glow. He would take the boy with him! His feelings for David confused him. He had already acknowledged that he reminded him of his own dear brother: Adel had always looked up to him and Hans had had protected him for a long time until he suffered that an untimely, painful death. Yet, saving David would not bring Adel back, and it was ludicrous to take him along—to risk his own life, the lives of his men and possibly the entire mission to save one little Jewish boy he had just met weeks before. Hans decided to stay away from David until he devised a way to bring him along safely, without jeopardizing the entire mission.

Very early next morning, Hans presented the commanding officer with a list of things he would need to carry out the assignment; men, safe-conduct passes, trunks, wooden crates, trucks, and weapons. He explained that once they arrived at the station, the soldiers would load the freight onto the train and then accompany the precious plunder to Berlin, while remaining constantly prepared to defend against enemy attacks. The preparations should not take more than two days.

For the next two days, Hans barely spoke a word while David, with a twinge of sadness in his eyes, kept to his duties polishing shoes and boots and cleaning out rooms.

The arrangements were made under Hans' supervision. Several convoys of trucks would leave different cities and converge at the station. The train would traverse Poland and cross Germany before reaching Berlin, where they were to deliver part of the booty. Hans' job was to transport the rest of the plunder to a naval base in northern Germany and then ship the remaining treasure away by submarine to its final destination: South America.

The night before their departure, when Hans returned to his bedroom, his instincts warned him that someone else was there. He flicked the light on, simultaneously drawing his gun. He heard a muffled noise, as if someone was hiding behind the door. With a quick gesture, Hans pulled David out of the shadows. Relieved, Hans scolded him for hiding that way, telling him he could have been shot. David just stared at him, frightened and sad. The sight of the boy, looking so miserable and now weeping silently, once again brought back images of his feverish younger brother dying in his mother's arms. He unexpectedly took David in his arms on an uncontainable impulse, trying to comfort him. The boy started sobbing but managed to say, "Why are you angry with me? What is happening?"

Hans answered quickly in a low tone, "Don't say anything to anybody. I'm leaving and I'm taking you with me. We're getting out of here!"

David could hardly believe his ears! He looked up at Hans with a sudden gleam of hope in his eyes, ready to accept all of his instructions, but it was already late, so he had to get back to his quarters before the guards arrived for the nightly roll-call. Racing back with the fresh energy of anticipation, he slipped into his cot, just as the guards appeared.

As he lay there, he thought about his father and the Shepherd. Unsure of the date, he wondered if Yom Kippur had already come and gone. He tried to remember his father's songs and prayers. He also recalled the last phrase the Shepherd had whispered in his ear the day he gave his life in exchange for his father's: "Trust in the Eternal One; only He can save you. If the Son sets you free, you will be free indeed!"

Could Hans be the liberator? David asked himself, gleefully grinning for the first time in such a long while.

The next morning, he could hardly suppress his smile, thinking about the possibility of escaping from that place where thousands of his people had been sacrificed. How ironic: Germans were killing so many of his compatriots while one of those same Germans was helping him survive at the risk of both their lives!

The trucks were being loaded, and everything was going according to plan. Following Hans' instructions, David waited in the shadows, ready to slip into one of the large crates that would then be under his personal care. Hans was in place, watching his every move to assist him and personally close the lid of David's crate.

While the guards were distracted stacking what was left of the plunder, David carefully slithered into the designated wooden crate. Both he and Hans were acutely aware that if their maneuvers were discovered, both of their lives would be in danger. The narrow spaces between the slats would provide sufficient air flow for David to breathe until they reached the train station. There, he would be able to get out of the crate once it was locked inside the train's boxcar.

After a few minutes, David felt the crate begin to move. He heard the voices of the transporters and marveled at the care taken to softly deposit the crate into the truck that would take it to the station. At the station, he perceived the same caution to protect the fragile, valuable contents of the trunks and crates as they were unloaded from the trucks and taken to different freight cars. *Nothing like the harsh treatment we prisoners receive!* David mused, as he felt the gentle rocking of his own special crate that secretly ported the worthiest cargo on the voyage.

Through the cracks, David saw that some of the men had already boarded the train that would take him to his long-awaited freedom. An incredible sensation of happiness, not experienced for years, flooded over him. The only thing that mattered for the moment was that from that very instant he could boast of the best sensation he had felt in such a long time: He was going to be free!

He knew he would encounter many obstacles and difficulties, but he also understood that he must struggle every minute from that day forward to reunite with his lost family and keep himself far from any circumstance that might take him back into captivity.

The train had been moving for several hours, and David was cramped. His arms and legs began to tingle. Before going numb, he decided to lift his right hand in an attempt to push the cover of the crate open. Hans had taken the precaution of removing anything that was blocking it. He slowly pulled himself up, making no sound in case guards were around. A grayish light illumined the wagon through the slats, showing that it was still daytime. Although he couldn't be sure of exactly how many hours went by, the persistent growling in his stomach made him suspect that it had been more than just a few.

Looking around him, he silently noted that his body was responding slowly, an effect of his lengthy immobility and the bitter cold. The boxcar had been stocked full, so the space available inside was very small. David managed to stand for a few moments to stretch his arms and legs. Removing a chocolate from the interior pocket of his wrinkled coat, he unwrapped it and slowly savored its delicious taste.

In spite of his uncomfortable situation, David wasn't focused on his rough reality. He leaned back against the crate to concentrate on feeling the immeasurable calm that allowed him to relish freedom even more than that rich, pleasing piece of candy that was still melting in his mouth. He cherished that moment, which came in welcome contrast to the expectative tension that occurred the moments prior to his escape. He knew that insecurity could return at any instant when the train stopped and the doors opened to the uncertain future that lay ahead.

CHAPTER 5

"Path of Light"

"Happy are those who bear their share of pain and injustice; with time they will be comforted and learn to be just."

THE HEAVY TRAIN GLIDED ALONG the worn rails. Its gentle rocking escorted the lethargy that had invaded Hans, who was sprawled on a seat of the train compartment that had been prepared as his command post. He was completely exhausted. The calm of the moment allowed his thoughts to turn to his protected one, cramped inside that uncomfortable box.

So far, apart from several Russian planes that flew over them without any consequence, the operation was coming along smoothly, according to plan. The shadows of the night were giving way to the light of a new day, and in just a few hours they would arrive at the border between Poland and Germany.

The long convoy was heavily guarded, front and behind. Soldiers were stationed all along the train, protecting long lines of artillery and ramps covered with dark canvases that hid trucks and other vehicles that would be used in case of an emergency. Preparations had been made for any unexpected turn because the cargo was too valuable to permit its falling into enemy hands. A slight smile sketched across the young coronel's face as he began to relish the moment of reaching his destination without great difficulties.

A sudden gust of machine gun fire shattered his musings. Leaving no time to react, the enemy planes dropped a series of carefully positioned bombs that exploded along the entire length of the train. The locomotive derailed and went flying to the ground, with the rest of the cars following one-by-one, each crashing into another. Shouts of pain and alarm were heard all around as soldiers, completely unsuspecting, were hurled by the expansive shock wave of the bombs.

The minutes following the attack were endless. Hans, who had been flung from his seat, fell onto the ground. He quickly stood up and brushed off the dirt that had penetrated through the vents of the train. His adrenaline rushing under the extreme circumstances, he instantaneously assessed the damages caused by the surprise attack. Without losing time, he yelled combat orders which were to be swiftly executed in case of a repeat attack of the Allied planes. After an agile examination that allowed him to evaluate the incurred losses, he determined an urgent mobilization of the vehicles in working condition was immediately necessary.

The soldiers who were unharmed prepared the steel ramps to unload the trucks from the train and without delay began to reload the incalculable plunder. Some of the bins had been shattered, their contents scattered everywhere. The task was not simple and required precision and efficiency.

Hans took advantage of a moment of agitated scurrying among his men to approach the next to the last wagon, which had miraculously remained on the rails. Apprehensively, he opened the door and scanned the mess caused by the impact: Boxes and wooden crates had piled up, and fragments of sculptures and jars from one huge, wooden box that had spilt were blocking the lid of the crate that hid David. Hans quickly began to remove the heavy sculptures to reach his friend.

In a hushed voice, Hans called the boy's name, anguish closing in on his throat as he feverishly tore at the slats covering the boy's body. When he was finally able to open the crate, he found David slouching motionless inside with a thin thread of blood falling from his scalp to his temple. Without a second thought, Hans pulled him out onto the floor and firmly patted cheeks, trying to get him to react.

David slowly opened his eyes, gazing up at the man who had saved him once again. As David regained consciousness, Hans reassured him that he would be all right. He ordered him not to move and then left the wagon, returning shortly afterwards with some food to speed up his recovery. As soon as David could walk, Hans slipped him out of the train's boxcar and into one of the loaded trucks.

Some hours went by before the trucks were ready to reinitiate their journey. Their first plan had suffered some modifications. They would have to follow a path into the forest, where they could hide and thus escape any new attacks until nightfall. As the number of able-bodied men was greatly reduced, the commanding officer was obligated to take control of one of the vehicles, precisely choosing the one that was transporting David.

The shadows of nightfall had begun to blanket the trees as the caravan started towards its next destiny. Taking advantage of the complex darkness, they finally crossed the border at the city of Frankfurt, along the Oder River. The city was silent, completely asleep. Hans directed the convoy, which now included a truck full of wounded soldiers, toward the city's headquarters.

Once there, he made the corresponding reports to his superiors, who reiterated the command to march on directly to Berlin. Leaving the injured soldiers at the hospital, Hans resumed his journey with a reinforced guard on the road to what was presumably his final destination.

Hans and his men continued their journey in the darkness of the night, where they encountered diverse difficulties. German territory was in chaos: Allied planes had already bombarded the principal roads, forcing them to take side roads and country lanes to advance and great formations of English and North American planes would appear out of nowhere like bands of bees, dropping their lethal shells.

Hans and his men were able to see the half-destroyed city of Berlin in the distance. The transport stopped advancing at the city's suburbs, about 10 kilometers from the port of Brandenburg, which lay to the southeast of the capital. There, they found shelter in the shed of an abandoned factory. Hans ordered his tired men to take advantage of the moment to rest. As his men dozed off, he discreetly glided through the cargo in his truck to reach his refugee.

Hans found David overcome with hunger and sleepiness, unaware of his arrival. He awoke startled, but recognized Hans as soon as the coronel covered his mouth to muffle the scream that had escaped his throat. Both cautiously left the vehicle and hurriedly entered a wing of a semi-tumbled office building. They carefully found their way to the most heavily protected room where the remains of a wooden desk stood in a corner.

That daybreak, David felt that more than ever that his life depended on Hans, who was hurriedly giving him some final instructions. He was to wait for him there until he came back without emerging outside, where his life would be in danger. After several stern warnings, Hans quickly returned to his men, leaving David with the most incredible sensation of desertion he had ever experienced.

After resting a couple of hours, the convoy started again. They swiftly advanced the last few kilometers that separated them from their final destination. By midmorning, the trucks began to unload their merchandise in barracks that were designated for that purpose. There was a lot of movement as a new classification of the elements being transported had been ordered, and a new inventory by a large group of experts was underway.

Of all the experts busy at their job, the only one who attracted the coronel's attention was a beautiful, young, red-headed girl who looked strangely familiar. Her features reminded Hans of someone, but he could not think of whom. For several minutes Hans fruitlessly searched and searched his memory, trying to figure out who she looked like while his men continued unloading the trucks.

Then his mind worriedly turned to his young friend, for whom he felt so responsible and whose destiny had become distinctly involved with his. He still did not know exactly what his orders would be, yet he understood that somehow he was accountable for the life of this child who was so close to adolescence. He was certain that he could not abandon him to chance in this convulsed city that reminded him of the crater of a volcano spewing molten fire all around.

Absentmindedly, his eyes returned several times to the young girl who was busily sorting out the booty with the rest of her colleagues. Although she looked Jewish, she had not deteriorated physically like the prisoners he had seen in Auschwitz. The look on her face, however, reminded him of those sad faces.

As he stood idly watching the girl, David's face appeared in his mind's eye. He looked again and jolted up in his seat, realizing that the girl's features matched those of his young friend. He remembered

David mentioning a sister and even showing him a photograph taken when they were small, back in Warsaw. He impulsively stood up, and without a second thought, walked closer to the young woman who was taking inventory the contents of the trunks and boxes.

His mind was in turmoil, and with painstaking effort he ordered his complicated thoughts to be at ease. What was happening to him? What was it about that child that had softened him? And now this! He tried to draw away from her, but something inside of him would not allow it. It was as if an internal voice probed him, *Could you really leave without knowing for sure if she really is David's sister?* It would be wonderful for him to know that this sister was so close!

He finally decided to take advantage of a moment when the young woman moved away from the rest of the group into a corner of the barrack. He approached her, and without showing much interest, brusquely asked, "What's your name?"

The girl looked up, surprised at his question and apprehensively answered, "Sarah."

"Where are you from?"

"Poland. I was in Auschwitz."

"Is anyone left from your family?"

"I don't know. I had two brothers and both of my parents."

"Tell me their names," the imperious order spurted from the official's lips.

A chill ran up the young woman's spine. That question shot at her like a projectile missile that exploded in her memory and her heart, bringing back painful recollections. Her gaze showed a certain suspicion and pain that moved the young official.

She answered with certain sadness, "My father's name is Gabriel."

Her father's name was silenced by the thundering voice of the administrator of the warehouse. He called Hans to inform him of his new orders which would be, according to what the young woman had heard, fulfilled in the most urgent fashion. Listening to the men's dialogue as she continued to work, Sarah understood that the shipment they were preparing should leave Berlin as soon as possible.

As the minutes passed, a strange atmosphere hung in the air. Sarah, still not comprehending, replayed her encounter with Coronel Hans Müller in her thoughts step-by-step. The only thing she knew about him was his name, but his penetrating eyes had been nailed to her face as if he were trying to penetrate her gaze to find something undecipherable to her. The intense image was fixed in her mind.

She felt, for the first time in a long time, that something had shaken her to the core, pressing her heart. She heard the voice of the man again; very close this time, right by her side. She sprung back, startled out of her deep thoughts. She felt a wave of heat cover her pallid cheeks as she tried to hide her disturbance by pretending she was lost in the task of verifying the content of the trunks and crates.

"What were the names of your mother and brothers?"

The question resounded in her ears.

"Can you hear me? Do you understand my question?" he urged.

With a brief stammer, she began her reply, "My mother's name was Ruth. She was executed in Auschwitz. Elijah, my older brother, died in the Warsaw ghetto. He was executed by the soldiers."

With difficulty, as if the pain that tormented her soul had gushed out, washing away her voice, she softly added, "I don't know anything about little David. We arrived together at the camp, but we were separated. He stayed with my father in the men's section and I haven't seen him again." She turned her head away, the tears surfacing in her eyes. "I don't know if I will ever see him or my father again."

Hans stood motionless in silent surprise. The painful reply of the young woman confirmed his suspicions. That young woman was his protected one's sister! The presence of the control personnel, officers and guards made it impossible to continue the dialogue. Hans nonchalantly moved away from Sarah to avoid drawing attention and suspicion. Reflecting on this incredible find, he left hurriedly. The astonished young woman was even more surprised with his sudden attitude of false indifference, which had not gotten past her unperceived.

That night in the silence of the room she shared with other prisoners, Sarah could still feel the officer's closeness. His aggressive voice had a grave tone that was now clearly recorded in her ears, yet his steel glare had lost its coldness when it surrounded her in a soft, light sparkle that faintly reminded her of the tenderness of her father. The sensation she had when that man left her side was with her even now in the blackness of the room, accompanying her with a new restlessness that, strangely enough…pleased her.

CHAPTER 6

"Treasure of Terror"
(United in Danger)

"For the treasure you keep to last, it must be made of love, integrity, and honesty; these are coins that will never lose their value or their beauty."

T HE LIGHT OF DAWN ANNOUNCED the end of a sleepless night for Hans. During the long hours of his obligatory vigil, the faces of the Jewish brother and sister flashed through his mind. The compromising situation he faced provoked a duality of conflicting feelings: his warrior's instinct as a German officer told him he could be making the worst mistake of his life for taking them while his heart accused him of being a traitor and inhumane at the thought of leaving them behind. Abandoning David by unleashing him in this chaotic city would be even ghastlier knowing where his sister was and not running to tell him about it. He would have to decide quickly; time was running out. He was in as much danger as everyone else due to the ceaseless bombings occurring daily. He wondered if he would even find David alive. Finally, he decided: he must continue with his rescue plan.

In the barracks that hid the incalculable cargo, the officer in charge told him that a last-minute consignment of paintings had arrived from the east and was waiting to be registered in a nearby warehouse, so he would have to make a brief stop there. Upon arriving, Hans could make out the faint reflection of Sarah's hair among the boxes and trunks that populated the place he had visited the day before. The officer in charge led Hans inside and began to relay his orders: A truck had been prepared and an art expert chosen to accompany him to help control inventory in the new shipment. Hans couldn't believe his eyes when Sarah climbed into the backseat of the vehicle in front of him as soon as the soldier started the motor.

The officer in charge opened the door of the same vehicle, inviting Hans to get in the front seat. Hans secretly smiled with amazement. Something supernatural was occurring, and his plans took an accelerated turn in his mind, becoming tangibly real with this help of providence. What else could explain why, among all the experts, Sarah was chosen?

He must speak to her as soon as possible and tell her that David had escaped Auschwitz with his help. A whirlwind of ideas spun out of control in his mind until the voice of the driver telling them they had arrived beckoned him back to reality. They quickly got out of the vehicle. New attacks were heard all around the city; the enemy gave no respite. They entered a large room, which must have been the art gallery of the study center. In the scattered gray sunlight that streamed through the high windows, the group began to work diligently to certify the authenticity of the beautiful paintings.

Sarah's eyes were pleasantly impressed as the works of Renoir, Zurbaran, Rembrandt, Titian, Rafael and others paraded before her. She recognized the authentic signatures and marks of the painters on the canvases she had so often dreamed of seeing with her own eyes as she read the art catalog she found in Auschwitz. As she fingered the rough canvases lush with such beautiful paintings, the face of her dear father and the image of the antique shop where her passion for art was born appeared before her. In spite of the circumstances, she was enjoying the moment. She knew that this was a one of a kind experience and still did not understand how she had been chosen to carry out the task of recognizing and preparing these extremely valuable treasures that were right before her amazed eyes.

All of a sudden, her mind repeated the scenes of horror and death from the ghetto and Auschwitz: the grimaces on the emaciated faces of so many Jewish women she met in the frigid barracks, the children who died of hunger or suffocation traveling like livestock in cattle cars, and the prisoners who died in gas chambers, like her own mother. How many were there? Thousands? Millions? She was petrified by the deep pain brought on by the thought of so many lives annihilated. And for what? To collect from their spoils that gloomy, cursed treasure that had unintentionally delighted her just instants ago?

Several hours went by before they finally stopped to have something to eat. Hans covertly approached the young Jewish woman, using the excuse of handing Sarah her ration to speak to her. Time was brief, so the young official spoke directly and clearly.

"I have your brother, David," Hans began. "Don't say anything. I will tell you what to do. Don't be afraid."

Sarah felt as if a bolt of electricity paralyzed her body, but she had to hold back. Her long experience in captivity had taught her not to express her feelings, so much so that she kept her face impassive in any circumstance, no matter how painful or shocking or strange. However, the revelation from this young man prompted a sparkle of light in her eyes that only he could perceive. He did not insist on continuing the conversation. He must be cautious to not arouse any suspicion. He still had a few hours to casually approach her to inform her of part of his plan, which was becoming more complicated now that David was no longer his only protected one, but also his beautiful sister.

Earlier that morning, Hans had solicited all he would need to transport the cargo that was under his safekeeping. He had forged two false identities using the personal information from two of the young soldiers who died in the train attack a few days earlier to include two extra men in the group under his command. Those two men would be none other than David and Sarah, dressed in military uniform. The young woman would have to sacrifice her red hair once again, cutting it to be disguised as a man. The rest of the afternoon Hans found ways to inform Sarah of his plans in short phrases, leaving the young woman more and more astounded, although she didn't dare pronounce a word for fear of being discovered by the task control commander.

As night began to fall, the shipping preparations accelerated. The Allies were attacking Berlin, so an urgent deadline for their departure was set for sunrise. A large group of soldiers began to load the precious cargo into the trucks. Hans thought of David; he must go look for him.

He took advantage of a vehicle that had been administered for his use. He would go to headquarters to receive his final orders, the safe-conduct passes and the uniforms he needed to begin the mission of transporting the plunder before going to find David. He commanded his driver to stay behind to help load the trucks and departed alone. After stopping at headquarters, he headed towards the abandoned factory where he had left David in hiding. The dark of night had closed in.

A stretch before arriving, he turned off the vehicle's his headlights and motor. With quick, agile steps he headed towards the entrance of the destroyed offices. As he got closer, he softly called the child, who came crawling out from under the dust-covered desk. David hurled himself towards Hans and hugged him. Hans briefly mentioned his unusual encounter with Sarah, which perplexed David. Tears weld up in his eyes, and he bombarded the officer with questions. Because it was so urgent to leave that place, Hans only gave David a brief summary of his plan to take both him and Sarah to Germany as he tried to calm the child, who was anxiously interrogating him about when he would see Sarah.

Hans gave him the same warning he had given his sister: they must not show any feeling, not even speak to one another when they thought they were alone. David would have to treat her like just any other man on the crew. After his explanation, Hans gave David a German army uniform, which David hastily put on before devouring the food that Hans brought him. Hans handed him the safe conduct passes and the document revealing his post as Hans' personal attendant, both of which had been signed by the commanding officers thanks to Hans' cunning petition. They swiftly left the building and got into the vehicle that Hans had parked close by. Only a few hours separated them from their departure with the plunder, and they still had to rescue Sarah from her quarters.

Under the complexity of the shadows of the night, they advanced towards some sheds outside the barracks where part of Coronel Hans Müller's team was ready to march. As soon as he arrived, he inspected his men and trucks, ordering the captain who had been controlling the operation in his short absence to start advancing immediately.

The group departed with the cargo that, according to the most recent update in light of the upheaval in Berlin, would have to be taken by submarine to Portugal. Eight trucks began a direct march towards their destination, but before taking the pre-established route, Coronel Müller had to return to the art room where another part of his group was concluding the packing and loading of paintings, sculptures and other valuable works of art. In a few short minutes, Hans arrived in the same vehicle he had used earlier that afternoon. He got out, leaving David alone in the car. The young boy tried to catch a glimpse of his beloved sister, but the darkness and the incessant coming and going of men at work loading the last truck prevented it.

When Sarah saw Coronel Müller enter the room that had been emptied little-by-little, her heart skipped a beat, although she showed no outward sign of the excitement that bubbled up in her knowing that her missed and beloved brother was very close. As Hans passed by her, he murmured in a low voice only she could hear, "Stay alert!"

A gust penetrated her, piercing her bones and making her legs feel paralyzed. She was afraid that if she needed to run to flee with the officer, her legs would not respond. She counted the minutes in her mind as the strained expectation of what would happen in the following moments intensified. She saw the administrator of this part of the shipment and the coronel disappear into a back room. Through the glass door, Sarah could see they were arguing, although she couldn't make out what the topic of their discussion was.

The soldiers had concluded their task; the last truck was loaded and covered with protective tarps. Inside a small kitchen, some men, after signing the delivery instructions for the valuable shipment, were discussing the destiny of the experts who participated in this operation. The SS official explained that all of them must be eliminated so they would not speak of what they had seen.

Coronel Hans, trying to persuade the SS officer, insisted that he needed to take one of the experts with him in case anything damaged the cargo. He added that he still needed to pass through one more place in Hamburg to pick up a few more paintings and that he would need an expertise advice. Immediately, giving no time for the SS officer to investigate Hans' next move with his superiors or to find out whether or not he was authorized to take the expert, Hans hurried to look for Sarah and gave her a cold order to get into the vehicle where David was watchfully waiting.

His eyes were unable to distinguish individual figures well because the quick steps of the official and hurried silhouette that swiftly slipped into the vehicle with a single movement did not permit his discerning who was who. The vehicle driven by the Coronel took off swiftly, and in the darkness a groan was heard as a body crashed against the backseat. The impulse had thrown the thin body of Sarah back before she was able to grab onto something. They were already well on their way before she was able to straighten herself up again.

They remained in silence while Hans drove away like a man who was escaping. The trucks that were with him had orders to meet with the rest of the convoy in Hamburg, so the official quickly detoured through different streets, wanting to arrive before everyone else to sneak the brother and sister into his personal cabin inside the submarine that awaited them. He pulled out a small package and threw it into the backseat and commanded, "Put these clothes on and tuck your hair under the hat. You will have to cut it."

David, then certain of who the passenger in the backseat was, immediately but fearfully turned his head. The headlights of an on-coming vehicle lit up the interior and for a brief flash, he was able to make out the features of his sister. He looked at Hans, who seeing the tears covering David's face, nodded his consent. Sarah also understood that she had to be cautious, but when both felt that they had a moment of freedom to express themselves, they stretched into an intense, wordless hug. The back of the front seat threatened to separate them with every bump in the road, yet they remained firmly embraced, aware only the intense beating of one other's hearts that were bursting with happiness.

Hans, intently watching the road in feigned indifference, felt that something inside of him had also been profoundly stirred as they both sobbed and caressed one another, as if that touch were waking them from a terrible nightmare, reassuring them that they were indeed both still alive after five long years of separation.

Hans' red eyes and ruffled hair showed the marks of exhaustion after spending so many hours behind the wheel of the somewhat deteriorated "Mercedes" that has taken them to the port of Hamburg. They arrived at the pier close to noon. Hans got out of the car and walked towards the wharf.

Sarah and David stayed in the vehicle, where they were half-hidden and carrying out the task of cutting the young woman's hair. She dejectedly felt her red mane diminish until it became just a small mat of hairs no longer than a finger-span from her scalp. The other trucks would be arriving shortly, so David hurriedly got out and threw his sister's recently cut hair into the water. When he got back into the car he smiled. In uniform, Sarah looked like an attractive, young German soldier. Sarah smiled back. They were so happy to be together again. They didn't know what lay ahead, but for the time being, they enjoyed a slight taste of that forgotten state: FREEDOM!

CHAPTER 7

"In the Belly of the Fish"

"When the voice of the accusers is silent, one can hear the voice of the spirit, which corrects, absolves and is never wrong."

Colonel Hans Müller, orders in hand, hustled up the narrow flight of stairs that led to the bridge of the submarine. After a brief pause to catch his breath, he crossed the bridge where the commander of the submarine saluted him, military style. The commander noted the surprise on Hans' face as he smiled and said, "I expected someone older. I must say, you are quite young!"

A sense of companionship was formed in both men from that moment on. The coronel informed the commander of his orders to safeguard this shipment, setting out to sea with it as soon as possible to avoid any attacks the enemy could make by land to endanger it. Given the circumstances and the increasingly frequent attacks of the Allied forces, both solemnly recognized the risks of the mission.

The commander insisted Hans tour the submarine. He pointed out that most of the compartments had been especially conditioned to store the cargo. A second submarine had been prepared in the same manner to carry the rest of the plunder. The crew would be minimal because the alterations for the freight had left limited living space. Hans explained that along with the four soldiers assigned to the mission, he had also brought two personal assistants. The commander assured him the vessels were prepared to accommodate them, and both men agreed that as soon as the trucks arrived they would transfer the goods from the trucks to the submarine to expedite their departure.

After having a short lunch together, the coronel took his leave of the commander and returned to the vehicle where David and Sarah were waiting. He instructed them to immediately prepare to board the submarine, where he would hide them in his cabin before the trucks arrived to avoid anyone recognizing Sarah.

The blizzard-like cold whipped the faces of the young coronel's assistants as they approached the submarine. They wrapped themselves heavily in their coats, which for apparent carelessness, kept their faces half-hidden. Sarah was especially careful to salute while half-concealing herself behind the collar of her thick cloak. They walked directly to the cabin that had been assigned to Hans, with whom they would share living-quarters. He led them down the long, narrow hallway without saying a word, having already given them detailed instructions before they boarded. When he arrived at the last door, he opened it to allow his assistants in before shutting the door again as he headed back to meet the commander.

They were alone, but suddenly, all the euphoria that had seized them gave way to flood of apprehension. The claustrophobic cabin locked them into an uncertain destiny, bringing to mind a story their mother used to tell them about a certain prophet who found himself under similar circumstances. Only now they were the ones stuck in the belly of the fish, wondering when and where it would vomit them out.

Early that afternoon, not long after Hans showed David and Sarah to his cabin, the convoy of trucks appeared at the wharf. Immediately, hectic activity commenced and did not cease until the very last bundle was tucked away in the abdomen of the submarines. The men assigned to accompany Hans on this phase of the operation were distributed among the two submarines, observing the orders of the commander that both crew and weapons remain minimal to allow sufficient space for such an enormous freight. Security would be extremely tight, and they were obligated to remain submerged for as much time as possible.

Before disembarking, Hans called a meeting to review the strategy to be followed: they must avoid any confrontation with the enemy, whether by air or by sea. Absolute silence was necessary, so they would have to cut off communication between the two ships and even with their land bases right from the moment of departure: Each sub would navigate with total freedom of command until they reunited again at their destination. The orders of the High Command were top priority, and they would carry out this mission even at the cost of their own lives. The future of Germany was in their hands. Hans delivered letters sent by Admiral Karl Doniz that spelled out specific orders which revealed the upcoming stages of the voyage for each commander.

When the meeting ended, Hans retired to his cabin, longing for a couple hours of rest. When he entered, he found Sarah and David asleep on one of the bunks, completely exhausted from the emotional events of the past hours. As his body stretched across his own bunk, tension gave way to fatigue. One last drowsy glance allowed him to distinguish Sarah's beautiful face nearby on the bunk beside him. Her rhythmic, quiet breathing soaked him in waves of warm tenderness that his sleepy state did not allow him to detect.

Hans suddenly woke up alarmed, believing he had just fallen asleep. Sarah and David had also been driven from their beds. The young woman instinctively ran to Hans' arms before thinking through her reaction. A strident buzzing and unidentified vibration enveloped the room. Sarah's body trembled in unison with the noise, which the officer finally recognized as the sound the immersion valves opening on the submarine. They had begun their descent into the deep waters to avoid being seen by the enemy. Moments later, still surprised by the new sensation of tenderness that seized him, Hans pulled himself from the maiden's grasp as he explained the cause of the turmoil that had awakened them.

Sarah ashamedly apologized to Hans, who insistently reassured her no harm was done, knowing that her recent experience living in a city that was bombed daily had shaken her and stimulated her reaction. David had observed the entire scene but soon discarded the outrageous thought that crossed mind as he wondered with a smile, *Could it be?*

With the young brother and sister at ease again, the coronel headed for the command post where the commander informed him of the current situation. They had left an estuary of Elbe River and were traversing the North Sea towards the West Frisian Islands. The journey was unfolding normally, although they could never disregard any drawbacks or surprise attacks. The commander also noted that it would be necessary to emerge each night, taking advantage of the heightened security darkness gave them to navigate more quickly while they recharged batteries and purified the vessel's air.

Immediately after receiving the report, Hans returned to the cabin where Sarah and David were appropriately dressed in their new soldier's uniforms, waiting to hear about the new developments. Listening to Hans' account of the commander's directions, they understood that their time on the submarine could become very tedious.

As the days drug by, the boring routine kept them shut in the cabin, resting on their bunks for endless hours. Hans would leave without a word; something strange was happening to him. Sarah's tense expectation intensified when the young official was near. Her cheeks reddened whenever she heard his steps approaching, and seeing him enter the cabin sent a pulse of electricity through the most intimate fibers of her being. She didn't comprehend how she had become so acutely aware of the man who was admittedly her protector for the moment, but who had never stopped being her enemy. Her contradictory feelings produced a struggle inside her that sometimes blossomed into a new, half-hidden emotion. David, on the other hand, took advantage of this incredible new experience at sea to slip into any corner of the submarine he could access.

Each of the five nights that had passed since they left Hamburg, Hans would return to the cabin to accompany Sarah and David to the deck when the sub emerged. This night was no different as they headed together towards the observation deck. Despite the intense darkness, they could see the swaying of incessant waves that occasionally curled up and bathed the smooth metal covering.

A dense calm received them. They heard the murmuring of the crew, who were taking advantage of the moment to breathe the cold air surrounding them. Hans invited David and Sarah to walk along the frozen deck, alluding to the need to move their muscles, which had grown lethargic from the permanent stillness demanded by the reduced space in the cabin. David jumped from the tower to the deck to catch up to the men who were heading towards the cannon, which was constantly prepared to defend against any attack.

In the darkness, Hans took Sarah's hand to help her down. She immediately withdrew her hand, knowing that she could show no sign of weakness; she had to behave like a soldier. Yet that fleeting moment of contact with the Coronel's hand had flooded her body with a wave heat that even the cold wind sweeping across the deck's flat surface could not chill.

They both walked in silence on the deck, lost in their own thoughts. Shocked by his own reaction, Hans distanced himself a bit from her, believing she had drawn away because she couldn't bear contact with him. He knew that she considered him an enemy and was distrustful of him in spite of the circumstances that apparently had united them. Concerned about his impulsive move in taking Sarah's hand, Hans reasoned that he would have just dangerously exposed both of their lives had someone taken note of even a minimal hint of familiarity between them. How could he lose his habitual, disciplined control? He would have to be more cautious and control his feelings, which he still didn't comprehend.

A sudden brightness, barely visible at first, advanced rapidly toward the submarine. Confusion arose at the urgent command to submerge; the men who had been on deck hurriedly escaped to shield themselves inside. Within a few seconds, the hatch was closed everyone tensely waited at their posts.

Coronel Müller returned to the command room, attentively watching the movements of the commander, who was communicating orders to his men. They immediately, though momentarily, changed their course to escape fire from the enemy vessel, which had dangerously surprised them. The impact of a nearby explosion violently shook the heavy, metallic mass.

Sarah and David had just reached their cabin and were trying to brace themselves when Sarah was thrown into the hallway, crushing her side on the cabin door on the way. A sharp pain penetrated her left side and her elbow was throbbing from a scrape across the rough floor. Tears of pain and despair ran down her cheeks face as David tried to help her up. Suddenly, two strong arms lifted her and softly lay her on her bunk. A sweet weakness overpowered her as Hans touched her arm and with a grave voice asked, "Where does it hurt? Are you harmed?"

She felt like she was dreaming! His warm hands helped David remove the clothing from her arm, where a large bruise was forming on her elbow. Hans improvised a brace to stabilize her arm, but was unable to do anything else for her. They would have to keep it under observation and hope it was not fractured because Sarah could not be seen by anyone else on board.

Soon, they only heard the monotonous, habitual noises of the machines at work. The flurry of voices had quieted, and everything had returned to normal. Drained by the incident, Hans and David checked on Sarah once again before they returned to their bunks to try to get some rest.

That night, Hans was unable to sleep. He recognized how much Sarah's close presence was affecting his thoughts. Lying there, he still perceived the warm closeness of her svelte figure when he took her in his arms. He could not get personally involved with anyone at this point of his life; his mission was of high priority for his country! In a few days, he would leave both youngsters in a neutral port to carry on with his mission and that would be the end of it. *The sooner the better!* He tried to focus on that thought to calm himself, but Sarah's sweet voice quietly moaning kept him up most of the night. Fatigue finally overcame him when the rest of the crew began their morning routine.

Thankfully, Sarah's arm was not fractured, and once the pain subsided, she was able to move it normally. The days passed quickly after that night. Sarah and Hans grew more attentive to one another, as they succeeded at maintaining a friendly relationship. Sarah's fall had eliminated the distance between them.

The sub traveled tranquilly beyond the West Frisian Islands and entered the Strait of Dover. The Capitan called Hans and his crew to a meeting to warn them that for the next few hours they would be crossing the English Channel. Maximum precautions demanded that all the occupants of the submarine avoid producing even the most minimal sound; absolute silence was required because the danger was extreme. They would navigate at half-speed and submerge as deeply as possible to avoid being tracked by enemy sonar, which could easily detect them in that zone. The silence on board was only broken by the monotonous humming of the engines.

The next night, the periscope appeared on the icy surface of the sea along the French coast, opposite Brest as they left Gulf of Saint-Malo behind. No enemy vessel was in sight, and everything seemed to be working in their favor, although it was too soon to believe the danger had passed. Once again, the captain described their situation to Hans, insisting on surfacing because the crew was very tired and needed refreshment. Their wan faces revealed the tremendous exhaustion of confinement: they were at the point of desperation. They urgently needed to breathe a bit of fresh air because the submarine's air was completely stale.

That evening on deck, the entire crew inhaled deeply, trying to trap as much air as possible in their lungs, as if they could store it up for the following hours they would spend inside. Hans, together with Sarah and David, was also enjoying the invigorating moment after long hours of internment. Once again, David recalled the story his mother told him about Jonah, the man enclosed in the belly of the fish. Although the days seemed eternal, he did not complain. However, deep inside he couldn't help but ask himself who was responsible for all of this.

In a few hours, the sub had recharged its batteries and replenished its oxygen level. The short yet gratifying moment outside managed to relax the crew. When the icy wind penetrating their heavy coats became unbearable, Hans and his companions went inside. The warmth of their cabin made them drowsy, so they lay on their bunks to renew their strength. Each became absorbed in personal thoughts.

The sound of the immersion alarm cut the apparent calm. The noise of men running to their positions and the metallic sound of the hatchway closing announced that they were once more hermetically sealed inside the sub. They heard the captain's continued orders as they quickly deepened their immersion angle and changed course. Moments later, the air was cut off and the engines stopped, creating a total silence that lulled the three roommates to sleep.

The dull sound of the diesel engine of an English boat that had detected them threateningly reached the sub. Simultaneously, a series of deep-sea bombs began to explode around the submarine, which was shaken by the huge shock waves and tossed aimlessly off course. The narrow cabin where the threesome slept was in convulsion. Not knowing when or how, Sarah found herself in Hans' arms. He held her tightly, shielding her body from thrashing against the hard framework of compartment. David, terrified, clung tightly to both of them. All three united, huddled together in tense expectation of new explosions.

Sarah trembled openly while Hans tried to calm her with soft words spoken into her ear. His words were like a tender caress that deeply perturbed her heart. She lifted her face towards his and his sweet lips captured hers in a brief contact that turned her upside-down. Without leaving his arms, she trustingly rested her head on his chest.

The explosions continued to lash through the waters surrounding the vessel for an intense moment that seemed to have no end. A loud sob from David pulled Hans from his warm embrace with Sarah. Still stirred up by the emotion that had seized them both, they immediately turned their attention to David. Panic had exasperated the boy and it took the insistence of Hans' calm, affectionate voice to quiet him. Hans gently took David in his arms in an effort to instill courage in the midst of the noisy explosions and commotion.

It was impossible to calculate how long this new nightmare had lasted, but finally the noise of the torpedo's motor moved away. The voice of the captain broke the long minutes of silence that followed, ordering the engines to start and the vessel to resume its course, gradually increasing speed to distance themselves from their assailants.

Even with the Gulf of Biscay behind them, the long voyage seemed to drag on interminably. Sarah grew taciturn after her embrace and kiss with Hans, trying to stop the flow of affection for fear of suffering again. She knew that they would soon part ways and she might not ever see him again, whether she liked it or not. Besides, he was still her enemy! With this in mind, she dared not even look at him.

When the engines finally stopped, the mouth of Duero River received the submarine in the quiet of the night. They waited there a few hours until, sheltered by the shadows of the night, they slipped into the rubber boat that would finally take them to solid ground. Hans had commanded everyone to change out of their military uniform into simple peasant clothing. By order of Coronel Müller, the sub's captain resumed communication with land to contact their liaison officers on that continent. After a brief dialogue that confirmed their respective identities, they agreed to wait along the shore, watching for the flashlight signals that would indicate the liaison's position.

The inflatable raft carried Hans, Sarah and David along with the other designated men away from the vessel. The darkness of the beach welcomed them with its soft, damp sand. The shining lights of the city of Oporto welcomed them into the unfamiliar country of Portugal. Sarah dared not breathe a word. These could be their last seconds of captivity! The fish had finally spewed them out of its belly, through its narrow hatchway and onto this stretch of beach. The twinkling lights of the port appeared to announce a new path towards redemption.

CHAPTER 8

"Mission in South America"
(A Window of Hope)

"When a feeling overcomes borders and distance, it is simply□love."

HOVERING VERY CLOSE TO THE shore and still encompassed by darkness, they distinguished the rhythmic, flickering code of lights they had agreed upon as a signal. The liaison was waiting for them. Sarah and David felt they were finally coming out of their nightmare. As their feet touched the sand, Sarah lifted her face heavenward to give thanks to the Eternal One. A prayer, unperceivable to those around her, flowered on her lips as silent tears ran freely down her cheeks. She covered her face to avoid being seen by Hans and the other men.

Hans was still suspicious because he was not acquainted with the territory or the person they were supposed to meet, so he warned the rest of the group to silently wait for him at the edge of the beach while he cautiously headed towards the figure that was watching them in the darkness. Just a few yards away from the person lurking in the shadows, he began the exchange of passwords. Assured of having made safe contact with the liaison, he motioned for the rest of the group to advance.

They discreetly approached the man, without delay or words. He walked them towards the first line of buildings on the outskirts of the port before taking them down a poorly-lit, solitary alley that led away from the coastline. Ignoring the new dangers they faced, the group followed the liaison officer, who was swiftly guiding them. They shielded themselves under the shadows to avoid being recognized by the few people that passed by.

In a few minutes, they found themselves in front of the humble façade of a low building with a narrow doorway. Passing through its wooden frame, they found themselves in a hallway that led them to a wide, well-lit courtyard surrounded by several rooms. After a few minutes of suspense, someone approached the fearful brother and sister to show them to their rooms.

The liaison officer invited Hans to follow him to a room where a group of men were at work on a large communication apparatus. As he glanced around, he was shocked to identify the presence of two familiar people. First was "Josef Mengele", the unforgettable "Angel of Death" doctor, whose face and name were forever engraved on his memory in association with death and horror. The other man was no less pernicious: "Martin Bormann", Hitler's private secretary. Mengele smiled when he recognized Hans and introduced him to Bormann. They proceeded to inform him that from this moment on, he would be in charge of "Operation South", transporting the freight of confiscated goods to South America. For now, he would remain in the city until the shipment was complete.

Arrangements were being made for Mengele and Bormann to leave Europe, where their lives were at risk. That very night, they were to initiate their escape using the same submarine that brought Hans to Oporto. Hans spoke with the sub's captain by radio, indicating the new instructions received and the change of direction the mission was taking. He transmitted the latitude and longitude where the provisions tanker would meet the submarine for fueling prior to setting course towards their new destination: the South Atlantic.

Before finalizing the meeting, the need to safeguard the rest of the shipment, which was due to arrive in Portugal within a few days, was reiterated. They must keep it from danger and above all, from falling into enemy hands. To do so, they would stay on land as little as possible and be constantly prepared for immediate evacuation should the need arise, taking extreme care to avoid arousing suspicion with the native people. Hans and all of his companions would have to change their identities to successfully complete the rest of the mission.

While Hans attended the meeting, Sarah and David found themselves, for the first time after many years, in a bedroom that had been especially designated for them. Although the accommodations were simple, they felt they were in one of the world's best hotels! Two large beds with white sheets and colorful quilts welcomed them. A door on the side wall of the room opened to something they had not seen in years: a sparkling clean bathroom with an enormous bathtub inviting them to soak in a warm, comforting bath.

What most moved them, however, was not the seeming luxury of their spacious, sanitary surroundings. They only briefly scanned the place before they looked at one another and, without pronouncing a word, stretched into a profound embrace. The tears, held back for so long, ran freely down their cheeks as they intuitively returned in their minds to the last night their family was together. A soft melody echoed in their minds then faintly sprang forth onto their lips, "Peace be upon you, peace be with you...always peace." Their whispered tune moved them presently as it had when they still felt their parent's warm embrace. Steps approaching the door transported them to back to reality. Sarah prepared for a bath while David bounced happily on the bed, and the steps continued their march past the door and into the distance.

Sarah sunk into the clear bath water. She enjoyed its caressing warmth on her skin as it soaked her body's parched cells. She took the sponge and soap from the shelf by the faucet and slowly lathered her arms and legs, wishing the bubbles could also wash away the invisible marks of all that she had experienced during the past five years. Her mind wandered between her past suffering and uncertain present. She knew changes had occurred both in her heart and in her body: she was no longer the same scared fifteen year old girl that entered the Warsaw Ghetto. The cooling water forced her out of the tub, where she quickly wrapped herself in a soft towel.

As she approached the full-length mirror hanging on the bathroom wall, she saw a young woman with short red hair and bright green eyes approaching. She stopped and stared at herself. It had been years since she had taken such a long look in the mirror. Her figure had changed.

She had grown into a twenty-year-old woman! The impact of that realization overwhelmed her and excited her at the same time.

An unexpected sound from the opposite door startled her, drawing her attention for the first time to a second entrance to the bathroom. A well-known, slender figure appeared in the doorway, gazing at her in astonishment and admiration. "Coronel Müller!" was all the frightened damsel could utter.

His full intention was to apologize and withdraw, but as though drawn by magnetic forces, he moved towards her and, without a word, embraced her. She responded to his sweeping caress with a relentless kiss, opening her lips to his while helplessly wrapping her arms around his neck. Hans, stunned and speechless, pulled himself away from her and hastily took his leave, closing the door behind him. Hesitantly, she returned to the bedroom, unsure of what to think. Not wanting David to perceive her flustered state, she put on a cheerful smile even though the fire of Hans' lips was still burning on her own.

Hans brooded on his bed for a long while after the staggering bathroom incident. How could he allow himself to be subdued by Sarah's suggestive beauty and tender response to the instinctive kiss that united them? The night was endless as contradicting thoughts circled wildly in his mind. He could no longer deny that he was in love with that young Jewish woman who had captivated his heart with her thin face, red hair and incredible green eyes that gleamed with a transparent light that reflected the purity of her soul.

He was amazed at how strongly this feeling possessed him. He longed to hold her in his arms again, but at the same time, he remembered what forced him to let her go and walk away: He was German. Rejection was inevitable because she couldn't possibly accept an enemy in the long run. Besides, he wasn't in a position to make commitments in his life right now with anyone or to anything. He had to fulfill the mission his superiors had entrusted to him: the gold and works of art under his safekeeping must arrive at their destiny. He had to resist! With the help of his military temperament, he would find a way out. Exhaustion finally overcame him, allowing him to sleep.

The next morning while the brother and sister still slept, Hans procured new, forged identities for himself and his men. What he really sought was to rid himself of Sarah and David as soon as possible to free his mind for the task at hand. With new documentation, they would be able to work and travel, to carry on with their lives as they saw fit.

When Hans arrived at their room, Sarah and David received him enthusiastically. Their faces reflected expectation. They knew that this day would change the course of their lives. He entered, enunciating a dry greeting as he walked towards the bedroom. Sarah and David observed his curious coldness attentively. When he stopped, he spun on his heels, and looked directly at them with a stern gesture.

"You both must leave this place. Your lives are in danger here and your presence exposes me as well." His voice was grave and his eyes were fixed on the young woman, taking note of her every reaction. "I have personally made arrangements for you in another boardinghouse here. It is comfortable and you will have what you need. Several months' rent has been paid in advance to allow you time to decide what to do."

Sarah's face turned pale, "Why have you gone to so much trouble for us?"

Without answering, he headed towards the door. Before leaving, he turned his head and said, "You have ten minutes. I'll be waiting for you outside to take you to your new home." He forced a half-smile and left, closing the door softly behind him.

Hans waited in an old vehicle, dressed in civilian clothes that made him more handsome than ever. He drove the young fugitives through Porto's unfamiliar streets. Sarah sat next to Hans, glancing at him frequently from the corner of her eye in an attempt to carve the features of the man she loved in her memory. The endless hours she spent awake that past night confirmed her love for the man who indifferently drove them through the cobblestoned streets of Portugal.

The picturesque shades of the houses with their different styles of construction momentarily distracted her thoughts from Hans, and when the vehicle came to a stop, they found themselves in front of a white house with small, barred windows whose frames were painted green and whose glass sparkled in the sunlight. Hans got out of the vehicle and invited Sarah and David to do the same. No one spoke a word, introspectively absorbed in their own thoughts.

A pleasant-looking, plump woman appeared and welcomed them with a smile. She greeted them in an unknown language and motioned them to follow her down a cozy hall plentifully populated with lush plants. She stopped in front of a tall, white, double-paneled door, which she opened wide to make way for the new arrivals. David smiled his satisfaction; he already liked his new residence, although he was concerned about not knowing the language the woman who received them spoke.

Sarah followed Hans into the room. It was very large and bright. The sun shimmered through the windows, invading the space with light. Everything was new, full of life and color for them. *I should feel so very happy,* the young woman thought as a tight pain gripped her throat, thwarting any response to the official's question.

"Do you like it?"

"It is very beautiful!" David intercepted, "I didn't expect so much!" He smiled with gratitude, as he headed outside to explore the rest of the house.

Hans stopped him and explained that they would have to learn Portuguese to communicate with their neighbors and find work. The house's proprietor would introduce them to a language professor who lived in the building.

"Do you think it will take us long to learn?" the boy inquired happily.

"I don't think so. You're both smart!" Hans replied glancing again at the attractive young woman.

"Don't you have anything to say?" David scolded Sarah, who remained motionless and silent.

Without looking at Hans, she responded, "Yes, it is lovely. You shouldn't have spent so much on us."

"I couldn't abandon you to the streets after all you've been through," he retorted with a dry expression.

A long, awkward silence followed. None of them were ready to face the inevitable good-bye. They would never admit it, but having survived so many persecutions and dangerous experiences together, they had become very close, closer than they acknowledged. Taking control of the moment, but feeling that something inside him shattered, Hans broke the heavy silence, "You'll have to wait a couple of days for your new papers. Once you have them, you'll be able to do whatever you want: travel, work, study...."

He made his way towards the door. Sarah tried to move to stop him, but her arms fell heavily at her side.

David asked, "When will you come back?"

"I don't know. I must complete my mission as soon as possible." After a thoughtful pause, he continued calmly. "I must ask one more favor of you."

"What is it?" David asked.

"Never tell anyone how I helped you."

David interjected, "But you saved our lives! We could never thank you enough..."

"It is necessary for my own good," Hans interrupted. "Now, don't speak of me. Don't tell anyone about me or the cargo that I guard. Let this be our oath of silence." He looked intently at David first, then Sarah. "Will you do this for me?"

At these words, the tension of the moment gave way to a free flow of emotions among the three. David, sniffling, threw his arms around Hans, who held him tightly, unable swallow the lump forming in his throat. Sarah approached him as well, eyes full of tears, and silently tightened her arms around them both. The quiet embrace had once again broken the coronel's resistance. Sarah and David, knowing that their liberator had concluded his task, tearfully acknowledged that they owed him their lives, which as their father had often told them, were more valuable than all the gold in the world.

Hans, unable to contain himself any longer, drew himself from their arms and left quickly. His heart was beating uncontrollably from the closeness of that young woman who would forever be an inerasable memory of an impossible love. Turning the key in the ignition of the old car, he glanced towards the house once again before driving away.

Back in their room, David and Sarah continued to weep silently. They closed the doors of the room slowly, as if by closing them, they also closed the door to a season of horror and suffering. The difficult chapter of their lives that began that Yom Kippur in 1940 was coming to an end.

In spite of the ache caused by saying good-bye to their protector, they felt that their freedom was reaching completion. They had survived despite the countless deaths around them and the dangerous flight that brought them to Portugal. Perhaps some distant day, forgetfulness would heal the wounds of their souls. Perhaps one day, they would forgive. Only Adonai could wipe away the scars of their sorrow and restore peace to their hearts. The thought of the future brought them a new aurora of hope.

As the days passed, each new dawn brought fresh expectations for the young woman. The secret illusion held in the depths of her heart was the return of her beloved, and she constantly envisioned the moment they would meet again. In the intimacy of her room, she elevated a prayer each night, asking God to direct her future, to guard her brother and to hasten the minutes until the moment she would be reunited with Hans.

She dreamed of the sweet kiss that would seal their lips and their souls, wondering if Hans anticipated that moment as much as she did. In the long hours she spent daydreaming, she created fantasies of varied scenes of their passionate encounter until, little by little, a sad disappointment began to reflect in her dreamy eyes. David entertained himself outside with the other boys who lived in the house, leaving her alone for hours on end, and although they both had started Portuguese classes, they were barely able to distract her mind from the dear memory of Hans.

One afternoon, she sat gazing at the violet hues the sunset was painting in the horizon through the crystal of her window. A book she had borrowed to become familiar with the language and customs of Portugal had fallen, abandoned, onto her lap. She gloomily admitted she was wrong to believe that the young German officer could be in love with her. Silent tears slid from her eyes and a painful sob escaped her lips. She had lost so much love in such a little time! The memories still grieved her, and strangely enough, especially the memories of the time she shared with Hans.

Soft knocks on the door briefly distracted her, but the lingering images her family returned: her mother on that last day before entering the gas chamber, the separation from her father and David, and now....

The knocks insistently continued at the door. Sarah half-heartedly got up, thinking the visitor had to be either the landlady or the language teacher. But as she opened the door, the threshold revealed the outline of Hans' trim figure. Without giving her time to react, he took her in his arms, anxiously searching for her lips, which longingly surrendered themselves to his possessive caress. They continued, connected by their impulse. His passionate kisses raced across her face as if he wanted to absorb her warm, perfumed skin with his lips.

A light sound at the half-opened door snapped them back to reality. Breaking into a mischievous smile, David watched them without making a move. He appeared to enjoy this scene, as if it were something he had long been waiting for. Seeing they had been caught, all at once, the three began to laugh joyfully, Hans swirling Sarah playfully in his arms as David observed contentedly.

From that day on, Hans came to visit Sarah every day. The weeks that followed passed quickly. They both remembered the time they were apart, dreaming of the moments they would share: moments that became a reality each sunset. Dusk would find the lovers holding hands or embracing along the seashore on a nearby, solitary beach. Hans took advantage of the time they shared to urge Sarah to follow him to South America. She silently listened to his proposals.

Sarah and David spent hours talking about their future. Both of them were having a hard time adapting to the city they currently were in. Besides, nothing tied them down in Europe now except the promise David and their father had made to search for one another if they were able to escape Auschwitz alive. Their situation made it impossible to look for their father now, even if he had managed to survive. They lacked sufficient economic means to do so and returning to the places from which they fled would be like returning to hell itself. The very thought if it terrified them.

They discussed their possibilities, going back and forth between their desire to start investigating their father's whereabouts and the fear of remaining in that place where the language and customs were so unfamiliar, complicating their ability to make friends and find work. David concluded that it would be beneficial to accept Hans' proposal to flee with him to America. There, they could save enough money to later search for father Gabriel. In light of the circumstances, the choice was simple for Sarah: She did not want to be separated from her beloved.

The news from Germany grew more alarming as the days went by. Hans saw that abandoning the city was more urgent and necessary than ever and was anxious for the remaining cargo, which had been delayed due to the recent unfolding of events, to arrive. His life and the lives of his men would be in constant danger if the remaining cargo en route to Portugal by land were discovered by any of the military services stationed there.

The port, like a magnet, was attracting countless agents sent by the Allied forces to investigate any strange movement of people or packages. The power of the Reich had been annihilated in Germany and numerous "SS" officers had disappeared. Neutral countries were the compulsory target of the service men who untiringly tracked the merciless men who, according to the reports that had begun to circulate, were responsible for the most expansive genocide of history.

The messages Hans received were increasingly despondent. The horrendous reality of what he encountered during his short stay at Auschwitz multiplied in the daily headlines. Hundreds, thousands and millions of Jews had been assassinated by the decision of one small group of men, led by a calamitous ideal that he did not condone. German or not, he could not tolerate what had happened. However, his duty as a soldier obligated him to fulfill the orders sent from Berlin.

On April 30, 1945, the city was further shaken by the news that Adolph Hitler, together with some members of his closest staff, had supposedly committed suicide. According to the announcements on the front pages of the world's newspapers, the Reign of Terror had fallen.

Leaving Portugal was imminent. Hans ordered his men to complete the loading of the remaining plunder onto the Portuguese ship he had leased weeks ago. They had been filling the vessel little-by-little as they made provisions for the task ahead, but the ominous situation demanded leaving that very night. The ship's all-German crew, specifically sent to participate in this mission, worked into the dark hours of the night in preparation.

Hans arrived at Sarah and David's residence abruptly that evening, much earlier than usual, startling them. He succinctly announced the day's occurrences and the need to sail that very night. Sarah would have to dress as a man again, hiding her hair under a hat. Their decision already made, Sarah and David obeyed Hans's instructions without hesitation, making ready for departure.

The events were dizzying. They were living in a state of inertia that impeded all thought or reason. Sarah was in love with Hans and was anxious to remain at his side, no matter where or how. David's logical fear of being away from Sarah, now his only family, put an end to any doubt in his mind. They were united in a new journey that, this time, would take them to South America.

Close to midnight, the ship lifted its heavy anchors, bow set for the Madeira Islands, where a submarine was waiting for them. After the transfer of men and cargo, they headed towards the unknown land of Argentina. What a strange sound that name was in their ears! In the silence of their cabin, Sarah and David spent days imagining the future awaiting them in that far away country. Would they ever forget the torture they had experienced? Would they ever return to Poland? Was their father still alive, and if he was, would they find him again one day? Many unanswerable questions assaulted their thoughts throughout the journey, but one forcefully resounded above the rest their hearts: Would they ever fully recover that peaceful image of family they had lost that dark night in Warsaw that converted their delight into a constant, endless nightmare?

CHAPTER 9

"From Hatred to Love"
(Calm in Paradise)

"Live each day as if it were unique and don't torment yourself. Live thinking that what you do today will project pain or happiness for tomorrow."

SUBMERGED IN THE DEPTHS OF the South Atlantic, the submarine carrying the fugitives remained hidden for several hours, waiting for nightfall. The war, history's most absurdly tragic moment of darkness, that had cost so many lives lay behind them. The voyage they were forced to embark upon was long and tedious at first, as they had to avoid the Allies' pursuit until they reached the Island of Madeira.

From then on, however, they sailed peacefully across the Atlantic. Finally, one afternoon, the engines stopped just off the serene, sunny shores of Argentina. They were close to Caleta de los Loros, on the Atlantic littoral outside of an unknown province called Rio Negro, approximately 41 degrees southern latitude and 64 degrees western longitude.

A similar submarine had arrived a few days earlier and was waiting for them there. They formed part of a crew from the Nazi hierarchy that had been able to escape from a convulsed Germany. Other members of the group, including Adolfo Eichmann, were still in Europe, waiting for the first part to be established before joining them. They brought along the heinous booty of war, which they had collected from different concentration camps and gathered through the confiscation of goods and fortunes that were pitiably snatched away from Jewish families residing in occupied territories. They also brought along works of art and famous sculptures seized from different museums, including museums of their own country.

On the beach, the crews from both submarines were met by a team of liaison officers who transferred them, along with all the cargo, to the town of San Carlos de Bariloche.

The submarine's captain, in obedience to Hans' orders, withdrew from the coast and sunk the submarines; no one wanted to return to Germany to surrender. Several hours of intense work demanded everyone's strength, even Sarah's and David's. The cargo was quite abundant and in some cases, very fragile: paintings of Rembrandt, Renoir, Monet, Corot, and Titian; sculptures in their respective packaging; and chests full of extremely valuable jewelry.

As soon as the trucks were loaded with the bloody plunder, they quickly began their march. They followed the route laid out by the liaison officers, passing through the wide valley of Rio Negro, moving towards the interior of the province, and then heading directly for the city of Santa Rosa. The journey on the dirt roads was difficult, but by the following noon, the caravan had arrived at the established destination, stopping at a solitary spot where the only thing they could see from the road was an old abandoned shed. Hans and his men got out of their vehicles and entered an old granary, which would hide them from any one traveling by.

Some men had stayed behind, posted to guard outside and to watch over the trucks that did not fit into the shed. They ate and rested a while; then Hans called a meeting with of the leaders to divide the spoils before resuming their march. They had decided for each of them to take portions of the treasure to different parts of the country because a reduced convoy wouldn't attract as much attention. Each small group would be guided by a liaison officer. One group left heading towards Cordoba, and another went through the north of Argentina heading towards Paraguay. Hans, taking the largest part of the cargo, went towards Bariloche, Chile.

After long hours of traveling that left the members of the caravan exhausted, they arrived at the ranch where they were to hide. The property's owner was Ericka Weise, an Austrian immigrant who was a faithful friend of the head liaison officer who had received them: Captain Karl Dietrich.

After taking a well-deserved rest, Hans met with Captain Dietrich and asked him for a trustworthy guide and vehicle. He wanted to become familiar with Bariloche and its surrounding areas. The captain soon returned with a simple-looking man, whom he introduced as Ramon. He had been Ericka's foreman for years and spoke fluent German. Ramon shook Hans' hand in a frank, spontaneous greeting, a friendly smile spreading on his lips. His attitude pleased Hans and a warm current of congeniality flowed between them both. The vehicle they were given was an old "Ford" pick-up truck. After a few brief preparations, Hans told Sarah and David, his supposed assistants, to get in the bed of the truck because he would need to be in the cabin beside Ramon, who was driving.

The warm afternoon sun illumined the youngsters' faces. They curiously observed the beauty of the landscape that stretched out before them. Different kinds of pine trees, larches and a wide variety of cone bearing trees flourished along the hills that grew and elevated into gigantic mountains circling a large lake. The sun sparkled on its mirror-like water, reflecting the picturesque cabins of the local inhabitants on its surface. They were in the midst of the greatest works of nature their eyes had ever beheld! David pointed out each detail that caught his attention, insisting on Sarah's admiration. Neither of them ceased to be amazed at such a marvelous spectacle. They momentarily forgot all their concerns about that once faraway country called Argentina.

Suddenly the vehicle stopped at one of the town's typically steep streets. David smiled when he saw the lake from the hill. It seemed so close that he felt he could skim the surface of its waters by just reaching out his hand. Sarah gazed at it as well, envisioning herself walking hand-in-hand with Hans on the lakeshore. The voice of Hans commanding them to get out of the truck interrupted their imaginations.

Before their eyes, they found a pretty cottage with a hand-painted sign announcing it was for rent. Hans asked Ramon to find out how they could get it, so Ramon, with his customary diligence, went to the neighboring cabin and knocked confidently on the door. A woman from the town who heard the knocking appeared through one of the windows that faced the street. After a brief conversation, she indicated where they could find the owner.

They got back into the truck, which stopped just a few blocks away. Hans and Ramon both got out to negotiate with the owner of the cabin. Once an agreement was made, they made their way back to the ranch. On the way back, Hans asked Ramon to make provisions for the cottage, purchasing all that was necessary to install his general headquarters there the next day.

Very early in the morning, Ramon left in the old Ford to carry out his task. He returned around noon and found Hans in the dining room having lunch. He reported that everything was ready for Hans' arrival at the cottage. Once he finished his lunch, Hans instructed Sarah and David to get ready to move into their new residence straightaway because remaining at the ranch increased the risk of Sarah being discovered. Sarah took advantage of the moment to tell him about the insistent glances of Helga, Erika's sister who had arrived to spend some time in the country. When Hans heard about the suspicion, he insisted on leaving immediately.

The old truck stopped again in front of the cottage they had visited the afternoon before. Sarah and David thought it looked even more beautiful than the day before. Hans, quickly followed by Ramon, jumped out of the vehicle, insisting with a smile that everyone hurry to follow him. Opening the entrance door, Hans revealed the cottage's spacious living room with its enormous fireplace, already prepared with logs to be lit. Hans moved further inside while Sarah and David remained a few more instants at the threshold, pleasantly surprised. Ramon's presence hampered their expressions of delight, although when their gazes crossed with Hans', he recognized a warm thankfulness in them.

They all excitedly explored the house's different rooms. David's cheerful exclamations transmitted joy to the rest of them. When they came into the kitchen, with its rustic yet comfortable furniture, they perceived an inviting, family atmosphere. An enormous cabinet overflowing with pastries, chocolates, canned goods and lunch meats covered one side of the room. David had almost forgotten about the wide variety of rich flavors that captivity and harsh journeys had denied him. Now the pantry was teeming with them!

Upon the massive table in the center of the room, a bread bowl displayed golden rolls that attracted Sarah's attention. For a brief moment, she remembered her mother, kneading the *matzah* that they prepared during the *Pesach* celebration that commemorated her people's emancipation from slavery. She imagined the joy they experienced knowing they were free after years of captivity; it was the very same feeling she and David were now enjoying, not only internally, but also as a daily reality. They could begin a new life! As Ramon took his leave, Hans asked him to remind Capitan Dietrich about their meeting at the cottage the next morning.

The sound of the pick-up's engine moving away indicated they were alone at last. Sarah and David ran to embrace Hans. After weeks of suppressing their feelings, they were finally at liberty to express their joy! They laughed and sang and shouted, until David recalled all the good things to eat in the kitchen and skipped away to make coffee and prepare a snack.

Hans and Sarah, still holding one another, sank into a long, coalescing kiss, yearning to recover all the caresses they were denied in the past few weeks.

David announced that the coffee was ready, and the peculiar, enamored couple walked hand-in-hand to the kitchen, where they enjoyed David's delicious brew and sought out a strategy that would allow Sarah to leave manly clothes behind and reveal herself for what she was: an attractive woman. To do so, they would need to buy adequate clothing and recruit trustworthy Ramon as an accomplice. That night, after sharing a delicious dinner Sarah had prepared, they each went to their own rooms, exhausted from lengthy hours of bumpy travel in the aging trucks.

Very early the next morning, a knock at the door declared that Captain Dietrich had arrived. He and Hans spent a long while in the living room, discussing the plan to mobilize the treasure chests and works of art. They would have to establish an operations base, which would serve as a refuge in case of danger, in the neighboring Republic of Chile.

For the moment, Argentina had opened its doors under the government of General Juan Domingo Peron. He allowed them in the nation under "certain conditions," which included their remaining completely clandestine, concealing their true identities. The agreement also implied that in a not too distant future, an "economic recognition" would be paid from the very "circumstances" that had brought them to the country. In exchange, they would also be able to use the "special sensitivity of the government" to obtain assistance from bank officials to ship of gold to other parts of the world where the ODESSA was in need.

As they finalized their meeting, Hans and Dietrich decided to travel to the border that very day to acquire a ranch similar to Ericka's in the neighboring Osorno Province, as close to the Puyehue Paso as possible. They agreed that once arrangements were made for the trip, the captain and Ramon would return to the village to pick up Hans. From there they would leave with both a cargo truck and a pick-up truck.

Before departing, Hans told David and Sarah to be careful, especially in front of Helga, who would be coming to teach them Spanish. Perceiving Sarah's alarm, Hans explained that Ramon had insisted that Helga, his girlfriend, be hired for the task because she was a professional language teacher and that after all Ramon had done for them, he could not find a way to say no without arousing more suspicion. He comforted them with the reminder that he would only be gone for a few days.

For Sarah, the days of Hans' absence were long and empty. She and David spent several afternoons exploring the town and walking around the lake where the young man was finally able to happily run his fingers through the cold surface of the waters of the Nahuel Huapi.

Helga visited them each morning for their language lessons. When Helga was with them, Sarah felt that her every movement was under observation. At times, the scrutiny altered her. Even though she continued to use men's clothes to secure the role she was forced to play, Helga's insistent gaze made feel her more vulnerable each day.

One morning, the young professor asked her why she had such a strong Polish accent. Not even giving her time to answer, she went on to comment on her beardless skin and the striking color of her hair. Sarah got up abruptly and fled to the kitchen. Helga followed her, examining the young woman's countenance. Her feminine reaction confirmed that her suspicions had a good foundation.

However, the pain that radiated from the face of the young woman made her desist from her interrogation. She returned to the living room where David watched in confusion. Helga said good-bye and left hurriedly. David went to Sarah and tried to calm her crisis of bawling, which was simply the result of so much pressure. An incipient fear imprisoned both of them: Helga might discover Sarah's double identity.

The following morning, they fearfully waited for Helga to appear, but she didn't come back. Ten days had passed since Hans left and four since Helga's last visit. The brother and sister stayed in the cabin during the day, leaving only at dusk and just for a brief moment to refresh themselves in the peaceful beauty that surrounded them.

One night, when they returned to the cabin at dinner time, a penetrating rain had begun to fall. A glacial wind ran through the streets, compelling the few passersby to find refuge in the warmth of their homes. Sarah and David rushed their steps, but when they turned up the steep street leading to the cottage, they observed with terror that all of its lights were on! Sarah asked David if he had turned them out before they left. When he answered in the affirmative, they decided to be extra cautious, keeping their distance until they were assured the coast was clear.

David told Sarah to stop and wait while he advanced towards the window to discover who the intruder was. In spite of his command, Sarah followed him. The instant they stepped up to the window, the door flung open and a figure appeared on the threshold. The shock caused Sarah to scream and faint. The tension of the anterior days had broken her nerves.

Hans' strong arms caught her and carried her inside to the living room, where he laid her on the sofa. Between kisses and caresses, he tried to rouse her. She finally reacted and, seeing the face of her beloved so close, extended her arms, grasping his neck tightly as she burst into tears. Hans asked David why Sarah was reacting like this, so he related the incident with Helga, which had terrified them both.

Hans smiled and tried to calm Sarah's anxiety. He confessed that he had already spoken with Ramon, who was now his unconditional servant, and had confided Sarah's true identity.

David went to his room to change out of his wet clothes, but immediately returned showing Sarah a large bag. He opened it and started to pull out new pants, shirts, and overcoats which, in his ecstatic rush, he tossed all over the rug.

Hans smiled and took Sarah by the hand, leading her to her room. She escaped from his hold when she saw the huge quantity of packages that Hans had placed on her bed, running delightedly to empty them, one-by-one. Each piece of clothing she unwrapped was accompanied by an exclamation of pleasure and joy that comforted an exhausted Hans.

He enjoyed the impressions his gifts had made on his beloved Sarah, who smiling mischievously, threw some pieces in the air. Her face was so radiant that Hans passionately took her by the waist and pulled her to himself, enveloping her in a sweeping caress, while his possessive lips claimed ownership of Sarah's sweet, warm lips. For a long while, they embraced and kissed, their passion rising until Sarah reacted and fled his embrace, leaving him there in the middle of the room, longing for more of her tenderness.

Instantly Hans, still stirred, followed her to the kitchen, where Sarah pretended to be busily preparing dinner. Hans approached her and resentfully announced that he would not be having dinner: He planned to go to bed immediately after bathing. He left brusquely, crushing her with his reaction.

All night long, Sarah fought the desire to go in search of Hans, but the precepts and commands rooted in her from countless nights of listening to her father read the Torah helped her resist any attempt. Dawn was breaking when she was finally able to fall asleep, so although she had only slept a few hours, she did not wake up until after ten. An exquisite aroma of coffee infused her nose, alluring her with its invitation to abandon her bed and hasten to the kitchen.

She put on the beautiful bathrobe that Hans had given her the night before, and walked drowsily towards the bathroom. When she about to cross the living room, she stopped motionless. There sat Helga, who looked at her with a smile; Ramon, who pretended not to see her; and Hans, who gaped at her feminine figure, perfectly wrapped in her new robe.

Speechless, she ran to find refuge in the bathroom. She allowed the water from the shower to run over her body for a long while, giving herself time to organize her thoughts. She finally decided she had to go out and face the situation naturally; it was the only way she would be able to show herself as the woman she was in the long run. Summoning up all her determination, she left the bathroom and was relieved to find only Helga in the living room: Hans and Ramon had left to purchase more provisions because a heavy snow storm was threatening to confine them to the cottage.

Sarah noted that Helga, in spite of her friendly tone, looked at her inquiringly, as if she had a curiosity that was still unsatisfied. Anxious to know what Helga knew about her, she softened her expression with a smile and asked, "So what do you know about me? What has Hans told you?"

Responding to her frankness, Helga told her that it was Ramon who had confirmed her suspicions about Sarah. She knew she couldn't be a man because she was too beautiful and too refined. Once she was certain she was a woman, she understood her teary reaction the last morning they saw one another, but she was still puzzled about the anguish she had perceived on her face. Helga approached Sarah, took her hand with affection and offered her friendship, assuring her that she could fully trust her; she would not betray her confidence.

After a brief silence, Sarah quietly confessed that she was Jewish. She closely studied Helga's face, fearing she would spot a negative reaction, but she found a sympathetic smile on the face of the young professor who hugged her tenderly and said, "Poor dear! How you have suffered! Now I understand why your accent is not German!"

Sarah thanked her for her affection and comprehension, embracing her unreservedly. The sound of a key turning in the lock announced the return of the men. Sarah ran to her room to get dressed.

Soon after the surprise departure of Hans' "second helper" to Buenos Aires, Ramon and Helga made a short trip with Sarah to the nearby city of San Martin de los Andes. When they returned, they brought along an enchanting young damsel with red curls and green eyes. When she arrived at the cottage, she descended from the vehicle, and with a distinctly feminine gait, strolled up to Hans' entrance, where she was discreetly welcomed in. For many, long months, that same scene repeated itself before the eyes of curious neighbors, who not knowing the reality, imagined a variety of stories.

As the months passed, Hans' love for Sarah became more fiery and uncontrollable; his amorous requirements were increasingly urgent and frequent. Sarah had no intention of pressuring him, so she never dared to mention the word "marriage", and Hans was still unsure of whether he should unquestionably unite his life to the young woman's or whether he should let her go free. He knew that her life would not be easy if she married him and he did not want to make her suffer again. He knew that the love he felt for her was authentic, and he was willing to overcome any obstacles that might present themselves, but he still was not absolutely sure whether Sarah's feelings were as intense. Maybe she still confused her gratefulness for something more; maybe the feeling would not last. Under those stressful circumstances, their relationship grew tenser each day. One evening Hans decided to invite her for a walk with the intention of openly conversing about their relationship. As they walked down the steep street, side-by-side, Sarah foresaw that this conversation would be very important.

The pine trees that surround the place sheltered them from indiscrete eyes, and they walked together along the shore of the lake, the silver moon reflecting in the water. The complexity of the place heartened Hans, who was determined to talk about his fears. Sarah's face, illuminated by the clarity of the moon, glowed lovelier than ever.

All of a sudden he was unable to contain himself. He embraced her, pressing her ardently against himself, as if he wanted to melt her body into his. Taken by the uncontainable desire to always have her in his arms, he murmured with broken vehemence, "Marry me, Sarah!"

Sarah had been longing for this moment. The voice of Hans rang like an incredibly melody. She felt as if she were floating in the middle of a white cloud, raising her upwards through the air. Could one heart contain such joy? She had been dreaming of this moment, but now pronouncing a word was impossible for her; the emotion overwhelming her was so great she could not utter a single syllable. Tears ran down her cheeks, which Hans kissed away with an indescribable tenderness. When his beautiful darling finally regained her voice she softly whispered, "Yes, my love. Let's get married. I love you so much!"

The hours flew by for the love-smitten Sarah after that night. Within just a few days, they had prepared a private, simple wedding with the help of Helga and Ramon. They found a small church among the humble homes in their elevated neighborhood and spoke at length with its elderly pastor, who agreed to bless the couple. Helga and Ramon were the witnesses and the other guests included only David, the pastor and his wife.

When the anticipated day finally arrived, the witnesses waited for the bride in the living room together with Hans and David. The door to Sarah's room slowly opened and an elegant yet unpretentious bride emerged. Although she was not dressed in white, her apparel was refined and regal. She held a beautiful bouquet of multi-colored flowers, a gift from Hans. Her face was radiant and his shined with a smile of immense happiness. They received the bride with joyful exclamations then headed to the church, where the Pastor and his wife were expecting them.

Once the simple ceremony was over, Sarah and Hans said goodbye and left for the Angostura Valley where they had prepared a cabin for their honeymoon. Helga and Ramon sent them off with affectionate smiles and promises to take good care of David, who would stay with them while the couple was gone.

"David"
(Roots of Resentment)

*"When man is able to forget his grudges and forgive,
all nations will live in peace."*

THE LAST GOLDEN RAYS OF the sun reflected off the snowy mountain crests and slipped over the treetops, softly settling on the calm surface of the Nahuel Huapi Lake. The crystal windows of the cottages that dotted the mountainside reflected the iridescent light of the setting sun, creating a garden of radiant sunflowers. The awe-inspiring silence of the scene was only broken by the gentle lapping of the waters on the lakeshore.

David's slight silhouette contrasted with the wondrous natural beauty surrounding him. All at once, he felt his vulnerability, his smallness. From the lake, the country of his birth and childhood felt farther away than ever. Poland. Even the peaceful scenery around him could not erase the lacerating memories that still haunted him. There they were played, fresh in his memory as if they had just occurred yesterday: the war, the ghetto, the concentration camp, the pain, the smell of death, the abandonment, the solitude. The hidden wounds of his soul, so marked by the atrocities he survived, continued to bleed although his body had recovered.

David had grown into a handsome young man whom no one would have identified as the malnourished, skinny, twelve-year-old boy who once polished Nazi boots and cleaned the terrible torture rooms where so many lives were tormented and assassinated.

Almost six years had passed since he had arrived in Argentina. He had grown up, learned Spanish, gone to school, and made several friends. One of them, Carlos, had recently invited him over to meet his grandfather, who was visiting from Buenos Aires. When they met, the pleasant old man held the Torah in his hands. David was immediately reminded of his father, who had had so often read from the sacred book, and he felt that something had shaken him to the core.

Sitting motionlessly, he sought inside himself to comprehend the reason for his anguish. He began to analyze that gloomy portion of his past. Fear and uncertainty of the future had obligated him and Sarah to cling to Hans like a shipwrecked sailor would cling to a fragile slab of wood. They had no other choice; they had allowed themselves to be carried away by the circumstances that surrounded them. The more he considered it, the more he was convinced: There had been no way to avoid it. They were very young and very hurt; they offered no resistance because they were not thinking but merely struggling to survive.

Now he realized how terror had paralyzed their minds. Their only thought was to flee, to escape that terrible scenario the war they did not comprehend had created—a scenario that had not only damaged their bodies but also their souls. After speaking to the elderly man, David felt as if his intellect re-engaged, projecting an acute resentment that he believed he had overcome. The hatred he felt for the German soldiers who had beat him daily and for no reason burst forth again, involuntarily. The loathing for those who led his Shepherd friend to the "death tank"...

Against his own will, his mind had opened the door to the pain and a furtive tear slid slowly down his cheek. How he loved that man, whom he barely knew, who gave his life for his father's! He was the one who set him free, the moment he first believed it was possible to leave that place alive. His last words resonated in his heart once again, "Just believe, the Eternal One will set you free!" He saw himself crying at the threshold of the barracks, fed only by the hope of that liberator. He would have liked to speak with that brave man again to tell him how much his words had comforted him.

He painfully remembered the angular face of his father soaked in tears the morning they were separated indefinitely and the covenant they had made to search for one another if they were able to survive that terrible nightmare. *It doesn't matter how long it takes*, David thought, *I will never stop looking!*

The last image he had of his father appeared clearly in his memory. He relived the moment step-by-step. His father's hand rested tenderly on his head as his withering lips elevated a brief prayer imploring Adonai to bless and protect him until they would meet again. He shuttered as a smothered sob gushed from his throat. That pain he had bottled up inside for so long surged out like an explosion of anguish that had finally surfaced, unleashing the accumulated ache and suffering that he had held since his captivity.

So much pain was guarded in his heart! Rancor opened wide at the thought of those absurd, merciless men who caused the destruction of his family and so many others during those terrible, endless days of terror. His eyes wandered distractedly over the surface of the calm lake, and a sparkle of golden sunlight reflected in his tears. The color of the accursed gold produced a growing sense of powerlessness mixed with a repressed regret: Just how many lives had the treasure that Hans and his men drug with them these thousands of miles cost? The curse was still with them, hindering any opportunity for true happiness.

His hand promptly wiped away his tears. A new expression was seizing his reddened eyes; it was a shine of determination that drew his once distant countenance back. He must talk to Sarah as soon as possible; he had to explain his restlessness. He walked back to the house he shared with Sarah, Hans and their children: Esther and John.

They truly were a beautiful family! Everything would have been so normal if it weren't for the fact that, as he was just reminded, they still shared their lives with Hans, one of the Germans that had consented to the greatest theft in the history of humankind.

Those sad thoughts flew from his head when he arrived at the cottage that had become their home since they settled in Bariloche. When he entered, he was welcomed by the cozy atmosphere created by the stone fireplace with its crackling logs, fluttering flames, and warm air that wrapped the scene in a comforting halo. Hans and the children played on the soft rug, the cheerfulness of their voices laughing away the sounds from the kitchen where Sarah, without a care in the world, was setting the table to serve the dinner she just finished preparing.

David paused for a moment to admire the beautiful image of his family before heading to his room. He stretched across his bed, his thoughts wandering. Carlos and his grandfather had told him so much about Buenos Aires that he longed to travel there with them to start, with their help, a life independent from Hans and his sister. Above all he felt an imperious need to get away from the village, where it grew harder each day for him to accept that those bloody men, like Mengele, were living at ease after torturing and assassinating countless people. The worse thing about his situation was his obligation to keep silent.... Silence! How long could he go on like this? He covered his head with a pillow, wanting to muffle the ideas that boiled in his agitated brain.

A soft knock on the door startled him. Sarah's voice called to him, insistent after his prolonged silence, "David, come to dinner. Your food will get cold."

"No, thanks. I'm not hungry."

"What's wrong? Do you feel alright?"

"Just leave me, Sarah. I don't want to eat. I'm going to bed."

She decided to let him alone, but as she turned away, she asserted, "We'll talk about it tomorrow."

The next morning, when David entered the kitchen, Sarah was busy with her pots and vegetables. He sat at the table without saying a word. Sarah heard him coming in and turned her head towards him. Seeing how tired and strained he looked, as if he hadn't slept all night, she handed him a cup of coffee and plate with toast with jelly without even asking. Then she sat close beside him and asked, "Would you like anything else?"

David snapped out of his thoughts and sighed, "No, thanks. Everything's fine. Don't bother."

Sarah put her hand on his shoulder and continued, "You have never been a bother for me or Hans. We love you, and we are concerned about you. You have been avoiding us, like you no longer want to be with us..."

David interrupted, "No, that's not it. It's just that..." His voice quieted as he doubted whether he should continue.

"It's just that...?"

David sighed, taking his time to answer. He wanted to choose his words wisely to begin this conversation, but as he spoke they flowed from his lips uncontrollably, leaving an aftertaste of helplessness and agony. Sarah took his hand and listened in silence, well aware that David needed her full attention that day. When it was her turn, she began by saying, "You know how much we have suffered."

"I know how much you, Hans and the children love me. I love you, too. But there are things that get harder and harder for me to understand and tolerate."

"What things?"

"Certain situations that maybe I didn't fully comprehend before because I was so young. But now I understand, and they are more difficult to accept."

"But what exactly do you mean? Please explain."

David stood up and started pacing. In an exasperated tone looked directly at her, "How can you even ask me that after all we have been through! Doesn't it bother you to know that Josef Mengele lives just a few steps away? That monstrous murder...that repulsive doctor of death! No, of course you don't! You never heard their tormented cries! Women, children....our Jewish brethren! You never had to mop away their blood, their vomit, their excrements as I had to day after day! They were massacred without compassion!"

Desperate and on the verge of tears he continued, "Even now I can smell the nauseating stench of blood mixed with urine and feces. Just how many people were tortured by his vile hands and the hands of his assistants in their macabre labor every day! And you know what's worse? Most of their victims were Jews: like mother...like Elijah!" He sobbed in anguish.

Sarah stared at him, stunned. They both wept, David leaning with both hands on the table for support and Sarah cupping her head in her hands. Eventually David continued, "You know what hurts the most? Having to hide the truth...not being able to tell anyone in town who that supposedly inoffensive 'photographer' really is."

"Quiet down! Lower your voice; you might be heard. Hans might come!"

David, unmoved, raised his voice louder and kept on, "I can't! I'm tired! I can't take it anymore! I can't go on being a hypocrite who pretends not to get it! I need to leave or I'll go crazy!"

The thought of David leaving sent Sarah into desperation, "What are you saying? You can't go! You promised we would never be apart. Where would you go? You don't know anyone in this country!"

"Oh yes, I do, and you know it! I have friends. I'm going with Carlos to his grandfather's house in Buenos Aires. I've already made up my mind!"

Sarah, sobbing, stood up and tried to hug him. "Why are you doing this to me? What will Hans say when you leave? Remember how much you owe him. He freed us!"

David moved away from her, "I have considered that. I know how much he's risked for us. But I also know that the money he used to bring us and care for us, even today, is the very money they stole from our people! I don't want to live with that cursed gold. It will never let us be happy!"

Sarah rebuked him harshly, "How ungrateful you are! It's thanks to him that we are even alive!"

David spun around and calmly looked her straight in the eyes, "You believe that he saved our lives? It wasn't him! He was just an instrument in the hands of the Eternal One. Do you really believe he was our liberator? Even before I met Hans I knew that someone would come to help me! Those days of solitude when I begged the Most High to protect me, only one promise gave me hope: *YESHUA HAMASHIACH*, he is my true savior! Not Hans!"

Sarah reached for him again, and a hush fell upon them both. They remained silently united in a long embrace before Sarah tenderly spoke. "I love you so much, David! But I also know you have a lot of pain to sort out. I don't want to be a hindrance. I hope that this decision you have made and time will wipe away, if only in part, the pain you have been carrying. I hope you can forgive. And remember, even if we are not together, we will never be apart."

David wiped a tear from her cheek and, taking her face between his hands, softly promised, "You will always be my beloved Sarah. I will always remember that our spirits are bound by a cord of love that is greater than man's. We are tied together by the only love that does not change, that unmovable love that our parents instilled in us...the love of the Eternal God!"

CHAPTER 11

"The Curse of the Gold"

"The evil may flee to hide their wickedness, but the justice of God will always reach them."

DAVID'S ABSENCE WAS NOT EASY for Sarah. She missed their long conversations and strolls with the children along the lake, especially on the afternoons Hans was gone, which had become a frequent occurrence after the arrival of more Nazi assassins. Unfortunately, they had moved into a nearby cottage in the neighborhood, so Hans was forced to spent long hours away from home. To make matters worse, when he did return, his gestures were dry, and he even treated the children differently. Her husband's change of attitude concerned Sarah. That night, after putting her precious little ones, Esther and John, to bed, she decided to wait up for Hans, who would be arriving shortly. As usual, his face reflected exhaustion and worry.

As she served his dinner, Sarah asked him directly about his recent indifference. Hans looked up at her and tried to calm her by dismissing the importance of the issue. He intended to change the subject, asking about the children, but Sarah insisted that ever since those men arrived, she had noticed that he no longer trusted her. She reprimanded him. After they had endured such danger together, how could he hide something from her?

Hans slammed his hands down on the table impatiently, leaving half of his dinner on his plate. He stood and tried to leave the room, but

Sarah intercepted him and to blocked the doorway because they had not finished their conversation. She implored him to talk to her and explain what was worrying him so. She told him she had noticed how he had been jumping awake in his sleep at night as if he were a prisoner to a recurring nightmare. With that declaration, Hans surrendered and, taking her hand, led her to the sofa in the living room. Sarah took a seat beside him and tenderly caressed his hands and face, trying to encourage him to tell her what had been tormenting him at night.

Still reluctant, Hans spoke, "No. I can't. This time I can't tell you. I don't want you to worry anymore!"

But she contended, "What can't you tell me?"

"I just don't want to expose you or the children to more troubles!"

"It's worse if you don't tell me. I feel so insecure!"

Hans, still doubting, explained that the men who had arrived from Europe brought a rumor that Coronel Hans Müller was the leader who made the stolen treasures of the Jews disappear. Now there were Israeli agents, led by a Simon Wiesenthal, after him and the rest of the Nazi hierarchy that had fled Europe with the plunder. That was also why the rest of the group had arrived in Bariloche. Hans reiterated that his greatest concern, however, was not for himself or the other men but for the well-being of his wife and beloved children.

Something grimmer had him unsettled as well: The presence of some of the highest ranking "SS" officers at Ericka's ranch, among them, Adolf Eichmann and Karl Hanke, who had been appointed by Hitler himself as the last *Reichsführer* after Himmler's alleged betrayal. Suspecting that the Jewish agents were already moving through Argentina, they deemed it would be necessary to disperse in different directions. Dietrich had taken Eichmann to Buenos Aires, where he entered with a new identity, Ricardo Clement, and worked for a bank owned by Carlos Fuldner, an ex-"SS" officer and a current official of President Juan Domingo Peron. Ramon left with Karl Hanke to the border with Chile to hide him on the ranch in Osorno. The rest of the men were heading for Mendoza and Tucuman, where support bases had been established by the first group of men that had arrived with Hans. So far they had been able to keep the doors of the government open to them with the help of the gold they brought with them.

As he informed her of these happenings, Sarah interrupted to ask if he suspected that there could be spies around the ranch, following those men. Hans replied that it was quite probable, which is why so much caution was necessary when talking with strangers and even their acquaintances in Bariloche.

Sarah stood up nervously and exclaimed, "I suspected our peace would not last!" Wringing her hand as she paced in front of the sofa, she blurted out, "Tell me! Who lives in Angostura? He must be someone very important! Such a costly residence there, so beautiful and impenetrable! When we saw it from the boat on Sunday while we were at the lake with the children, I remember you telling me it could not even be reached by land. Will you once and for all tell me who lives there? Or will you continue to protect those evil men even from me?" Her voice rose in indignation.

"Calm down, my love. Please!" Hans tried to persuade his wife, moving close to her.

She backed away, unleashing her anger, "Tell me who is there! Caring for whoever it is makes you edgier every day!"

Hans fell defeated onto his chair and, barely audible, answered, "It is Adolf Hitler."

"No! No, it can't be! That terrible man! The wickedest person I know of has been living here?! Since when?" She paused. "You know, David was right. It is unbearable! Just to think that the person who commanded the execution of millions of people without any sign of compassion is now living here, at ease, infuriates me! How I wish I could speak freely! To unmask him and let him pay for his crimes!" Her voice faded, smothered by her weeping.

Hans tried to calm her down, but she forcefully tore herself from his arms and ran to the bedroom. A heavy silence fell upon them both. That night the nightmares haunted Hans' dreams again. Smothered screams crept from his throat as the enemy pursued and overtook him; they carried him away as a prisoner and subdued him to the terrible tortures he had witnessed in the concentration camp. As a pained groan started to shake him, Sarah gently shook him to bring him back to reality. Bathed in a cold sweat, he clung to her and begged her to understand that even outside of Germany he had to obey his superiors. He was terrified! Hitler presence there had greatly increased the danger for everyone, and they must be more vigilant than ever. Sarah rocked him in her arms, not wanting to further provoke her husband's altered state.

A week later, Ramon went to Angostura to bring back provisions for the ranch and parts for the farm equipment. Once his task was done, he went into a bar in the town to have lunch before the long ride back. As he ate, someone who had been watching him from a nearby table walked up and, in a friendly tone but with a distinctly foreign accent, asked about the young woman who had accompanied him there a few days before and went on with a perfect description of Sarah and insisted on knowing her nationality. Ramon, highly cautious, denied knowing where she was from and, feigning rural dialect, questioned, "Why do you ask?"

The stranger said it was just curiosity, he thought perhaps there were some of his co-patriots around with whom he could form a friendship. Ramon, fearing for the safety of his friends, said good-bye hurriedly, and left under the pretext of still needing to purchase more parts for his equipment. He drove away carefully, making sure he was not seen by the stranger as he headed back to the ranch.

Very upset, Ramon went to tell Hans what had happened. Hans was equally perturbed by the incident and went straight home. An incipient darkness had begun to descend on the streets, blocking the final rays of sunset. When he reached the base of his steep street, his instinct told him to be cautious, so he left the vehicle a block away and stealthily snuck through the last stretch blackness that separated him from his cottage.

Suddenly, the lights of the living room flicked on and Hans saw two dark figures approaching the cottage. Surprised by the light turning on, they quickly retreated. Hans tried to follow them but lost them at the next corner where they had disappeared into the shadows. He retraced his steps back to the cottage.

His agitated entrance surprised Sarah and the children, who were playing peacefully by the fireplace. The twitching on his face made Sarah feel uneasy; she knew something was wrong. She followed him to the bedroom where she found him searching frantically for a machine gun he kept on a high shelf in the closet. Sarah took him by the arm to get his attention and with urgency in her voice asked what was going on. Hans immediately asked her to prepare the children and enough clothes to spend a few days in the country.

While Sarah packed their bags, Hans went for the truck he had left close by after instructing her not to open the door for anyone. In a few minutes they were on their way to the ranch, but first they had driven around the town a few times to make sure no one was following them. When they arrived at Erika's ranch, Sarah and the children were shown to their rooms while Hans ordered the men to post guard, assigning both day and night shifts.

Sarah spent the following days in silence, caring for her little ones. Hans stayed in his improvised headquarters in the old mill, which also served as a watch tower for the road leading to the ranch.

Hans walked restlessly that particular evening, peering through his binoculars every so often towards the dark path that led to the house. The clarity of the moon changed the aspect of the terrain, drawing perfect shadows of the trees surrounding the house. All of a sudden, in the distance he saw the headlights of a vehicle detour from the main road and shut off close to the ranch's entrance. He nervously waited for any sign of the slightest movement.

As he coldly prepared his weapon, a figure stealthily glided through the darkness, moving towards the house. The figure craftily brushed past a dim light that flickered from the children's bedroom before disappearing into the shadows again.

Meanwhile, Hans had approached the man, startling him as he bashed him on the head with his gun. Without much resistance, he took him down and carried him off to the mill, where he tied him to an old chair and gagged his mouth with a cloth. Then he threw a bucket of cold water on him to wake him up. When the prisoner opened his eyes, he found Ramon's threatening pistol against his mouth. Hans' furious and investigative glare stared him up and down. After a few minutes, he pulled the gag rag out of the man's mouth with a single blow that brought a trickle of blood to his lips.

Hans's interrogation began, "You disgraceful dog. Why have you come here?"

The man, still recovering from the strike and aware of Hans' intimidating fist in his face, tried to explain. "Acthung! Acthung!" he stuttered.

"Where did you learn German? Are you Jewish?"

"Please, Coronel Müller. Listen to me!" the man implored between heavy breaths.

Hans furiously punched him again, his nerves on edge. "What were you trying to do? How do you know my name?"

The man replied, "I've been sent by Capitan Dietrich to look for you, sir. I have a letter for you in the lining of my coat."

Hans, still unconvinced, checked his coat and found a crumpled envelope which he quickly opened. His tired eyes read:

> Coronel Müller:
>
> The services have informed me that Wiesenthal's people are on the move here in Buenos Aires. They are after you. Your life and everything in your custody is in danger. Time is short. Coronel Eichmann recommends you speak to no one. Trust only the one he is sending you: Capitan Klaus Kramer, one of Goring's ex-functionaries of the State. His command is to support you in whatever it takes to remove the plunder from Argentina.
>
> Greetings.
> Karl Dietrich.

After reading the letter, Hans apologized to Capitan Kramer and ordered Ramon to untie him. They fed him, gave him clean clothes and told him rest for a few hours while he and Ramon prepared for departure with the rest of the men. They ventured deeper into the ranch's property to the silo where the cargo was hidden, taking two trucks to assist them in the task of transporting the plunder once again. Having learned that Klaus was not his enemy, Ramon took advantage of the moment they were alone in the kitchen to apologize for his earlier actions. As they drank a cup of coffee, Ramon asked the Capitan if he had had a difficult trip to the ranch.

Klaus answered, "Very difficult. At one point of the journey I was being followed. I had to run the pursuer off the road and find another one for my escape. As I drove away, I saw that they turned around the road's shoulder and continued towards Bariloche. The change of directions had disoriented me, delaying my arrival here at the ranch."

Ramon suspected that the man who had interrogated him about Sarah the day before was from that group. He informed Capitan Klaus of the incident, and both agreed that it was essential to leave as soon as possible.

Hans, before leaving to prepare the treasures for their next journey, had explained the situation to Sarah. They would have to head to the Cordillera de los Andes and cross the border into Southern Chile where they could establish their own ranch. Sarah asked in alarm, "What's going on now? Why do we have to flee so soon?"

Hans answered, "Wiesenthal's people are tracking the surrounding areas. Someone has assured them that some of the men they seek are here, above all the "SS" agents that fled from Europe with the assets we have hidden. They want to keep us from crossing the border because it will be harder for them to catch us in another country. Here they practically have us cornered."

"What will happen to us now?" Sarah insisted anxiously, "Are our children in danger? I don't fear for myself, but what about them? They are so small!" She hugged Hans tightly. He held her in his protective arms and kissed her hair as he tried to calm her fears.

Sarah then went to prepare their things with the children while Hans and Ramon worked out the final details of the evacuation of the booty. As soon as they were all ready, they began their march towards the border in their respective trucks. In a few hours they found themselves very close to the dividing lines. They had left Angostura behind and were about to cross the border at the Puyehue Pass.

Arriving on Chilean territory, they felt more secure. The imposing beauty of the scenery lighted by the first rays of daybreak welcomed them. The Villarica Volcano, like a majestic sentinel, reflected on the lake that lay at their laps. The landscape's vegetation beautified the panorama with its color. Despite the fact that they were fleeing, it was impossible to not enjoy that fleeting moment until, leaving behind the marvelous gift that nature had granted, they arrived at the spacious, flourishing ranch in Osorno a few hours later.

Once they settled in, tranquility appeared to reign again for Hans and his family even though they had to remain on the ranch as much as possible for fear of being recognized in town. As soon as they had arrived, Hans and his men had set up some equipment for a short-waved radio which allowed them to stay informed and maintain permanent communication with their countrymen in the different places they resided. They had also used that system to order a shipment of gold from the Official Banks in Argentina to banks in Switzerland, as the ODESSA had required.

For Esther and John, their days on the ranch were happy and entertaining. The young girl, who was the oldest, had just celebrated her sixth birthday. She and her brother, who was only four, played for long hours and entertained themselves watching the ranch workers. They were fascinated by the baby animals and loved horse-back riding with their parents.

That afternoon, Hans and Sarah were watching their children, who were absorbed in one of their games, through the window. Sarah again tried to convince Hans that it was be necessary to send the young girl to school. Hans stubbornly and fearfully asked her to wait a little longer until they were certain that no one was pursuing them. Sarah became agitated as both were trying to justify their points of view. Trying to end the discussion, Sarah complained that she couldn't stand the thought of her children living hidden away any longer. Hans wouldn't hear of it and left, slamming the door behind him.

However, Sarah did not obey her husband's warnings. She ordered a ranch hand to get a truck ready to take her to the city. There, she visited different schools to find out how to register Esther and went shopping. On her way home, she noticed a vehicle close the ranch entrance. Its foreign occupants were suspiciously scanning the ranch through their binoculars. She ordered the ranch hand to hurry her home and asked him not to mention the incident to her husband.

To her surprise, Hans was waiting for her, his face seething anger. He confronted her, accusing her of not loving her children because she was willing to expose them to danger, knowing how risky it was to be discovered by the members of the Israeli Service. According to the news Klaus brought with him, the Mossad was after them again. Nevertheless, Sarah was also stubborn and would not listen to his reasoning; she walked away defiantly and entered the house to look for her little ones.

That evening, the situation between the spouses was still tense, so Sarah decided to sleep in the children's bedroom.

The news Kramer brought coupled with the ranch hand's comments, put Hans into red-alert mode. He ordered his men to prepare the most essential items they would need to move their operations. The men were used to these improvised movements, so they promptly had everything arranged to depart for Santiago de Chile.

When Hans called her with the news of their departure, Sarah sprung out of bed, more furious than afflicted. She harshly reprimanded him, "Fleeing again? Why?"

"Don't ask. It's just necessary," Hans replied.

"Necessary! That is your explanation? Who do you think you are to lay out my life and the lives of my children without consulting me? You send us here and there like your little packages!"

"Don't you understand? Our lives are in danger!" Hans retorted both furiously and urgently.

"Our lives? What have my children and I done? You are the one who is fleeing to cover for those monstrous assassins and to protect that cursed booty they have stolen from my people. David was right when he left! The curse of that gold is going to haunt us our entire lives…!"

Hans interrupted starkly, "Silence! You don't know what you are saying!"

She continued hysterically, her voice rising in rage, "Or are you really one of them? A dirty Nazi criminal!"

Hans reacted violently, slapping her firmly across her cheek. Her shriek woke the children, who ran fearfully to their mother's arms. She sobbed in pain as the sting from Hans' hand pierced her soul. She sat on the edge of the bed, comforting her teary-eyed children. Hans repentantly knelt at her side to embrace the three of them, and on the verge of desperation said, "Sarah, you know you are my life. You and the children are all I have! Without you, nothing matters. Do you understand me? Your lives are the most important thing I must defend."

Having said this, he left the room, returning in a few minutes with a cup of coffee to share with Sarah. Sarah calmly told Hans she had decided to return to Argentina.

Hans despairingly asked her, "Do you think it's that easy? If you do, you are wrong. They're not only looking for me. They are looking for you, too. They know that we are married and they could take you or one of the children hostage, and I don't think you want to risk that for the children's sake."

Crushed by his argument, Sarah realized that she had no other option than to escape with her husband once again.

With the first light of day, they left the ranch. The group of trucks headed north. Hans drove the truck in the rearguard with his family, Klaus and Ramon, who had decided to stay with them permanently. They sat silently, watching the road they were leaving behind to warn Hans if they saw something abnormal.

The vehicles advanced without much difficulty until they arrived at the city of Osorno, where fueling was inevitable. When they approached at the gas station, they stopped several hundred yards before they would be seen so they could enter one at a time to avoid drawing unnecessary attention to themselves.

The first truck filled its tank and left unhurriedly but without waiting for the rest. The last truck to enter the station was Hans'. He had been watching for the other vehicles disappear out of sight. Within a few minutes, they had refueled and were on their way back to the route that would lead them out of the city, not noticing that they were being followed. As they left the last houses of the town behind, they sped up their pace on the solitary road. All of a sudden, they noticed something strange: A car was racing in their direction! Flying towards them unbridled, it slammed on its brakes, tires squealing as it stopped horizontally across the road, blocking it off.

Hans, with a great command of the wheel, spun the truck away from the car, plunging them in the opposite direction before skidding onto a secondary road he used to speed away. Seeing that his pursuers were still hot on his trail, Hans drove between the trees of the woods that lined the road.

Hearing the first shots, he quickly gave the wheel over to Sarah to free his hands for action. They looked for refuge among the tress where they waited, out of sight, for their persecutors to reach them. Without delay, they appeared at the bend in the road. As they drove past, Hans and his men would attack them full-force.

Hans and Ramon immediately repelled the enemy fire. After a confrontation that wounded three of the four attackers and shattered its vehicles' widows and pneumatics, they verified that they hadn't suffered any severe damages and swiftly drove away, returning to the original route to reunite with the trucks that were waiting for them in the place they had agreed upon previously.

Sarah gathered her children in her arms, trying to quiet their sobs. Ramon's left arm was bleeding; he had been grazed by a bullet. After cleaning his wound and making sure he was alright, they decided to continue towards Temuco, remaining watchful and precautious.

They continued north without any more major problems, having evaded their pursuers. Finally, after two days of travel, a dense rain received them as they descended into the city of Santiago, close to the Central Station of the Chilean capital.

A dark, old shed was the provisional refuge prepared by Dietrich to hide the vehicles from curious eyes. Hans decided to leave them under cover there temporarily with the treasures, delegating Klaus to the command in his absence as he and his family had to continue into the city. Fearing that their truck could be recognized by someone who might inform their persecutors, he was determined to continue on foot for heightened safety.

Hans, Sarah and the children followed behind Dietrich, camouflaging themselves under the shadows through the narrow streets that took them to the hidden boardinghouse. The dim light gave the room a mysterious aspect. An elderly man with a white moustache was sleeping on a shabby chair beside a stove. Sarah and the children were shivering with cold, their wet clothes clinging to their bodies. They waited in silence as the men went near. Capitan Dietrich called out to the old man by name, "Jose!"

Hearing his name, the man woke up startled. He stood up hastily and, recognizing Dietrich, smiled at the children and led them into the next room. Before long a short, plump woman named Martha appeared. She took Sarah and the children to their room, directing them down narrow hallway, at the end of which she stopped to withdraw a large ring of keys and opened the door for the recent arrivals. Straight away, Sarah undressed the children and gave them into a warm bath with Martha's help. Esther and John had a glass of milk and some cookies before, exhausted from the journey and relaxed by the warm bath, falling peacefully asleep in the room adjoining that of their parents. Sarah thanked Martha for her help. Martha in turn smiled as she left the room to give Sarah some much needed privacy.

Sarah had been longing to soak away the dust and weariness of the trip since shortly after leaving home. She removed her damp clothes and unwound as she unbraided her long red locks in front of the bathroom mirror. She noted that the marks of fatigue reflecting back at her gave her face a special splendor, a touch that only maturity and experience bestowed. She had lost weight, which was just as clear in the image of her body in the mirror as in the loose appearance of her once fitted garments.

Thinking only of the delight of the moment, she stepped into the bathtub, savoring the comforting sensation of warmth that caressed her body and intimately stirred her. She closed her beautiful emerald eyes and relaxed, allowing her mind to wander to what seemed to be a distant memory: How long had it been since she made love to her husband? As if responding to her silent call, Hans appeared at the threshold of the door and watched her for a few moments.

Unbeknownst to Sarah, he was asking himself the same question. He quietly undressed, so as not to draw her attention, and then tiptoed behind her, administering a soothing massage to her tired neck and shoulders before sliding into the bathtub with her. It had been so long since they had been intimate that both were flooded by a fire that was impossible to control. Hans carried Sarah to their bed, where they were united in an embrace of desperate love.

The next morning, a discreet knock at the door woke Hans up. He covered Sarah, jumped from his bed and half-opened the door to find Martha's round face announcing that breakfast was served. Dietrich and Ramon were waiting for him. When Hans entered the kitchen, he found the men studying a map of Santiago. Seeing Hans, Dietrich described the need to get a new vehicle to travel safely within the city.

Hans explained his need of finding a house near the capital, in a peaceful neighborhood where Sarah and the children could live serenely. Dietrich informed him that there should be no problem: They had the protection of the current government as arrangements had gone into effect in Mendoza, under the protection of General Carlos Ibanez del Campo. With his endorsement they could move freely to search for a new home. A few days later, Hans took Sarah to a huge, extraordinarily gorgeous house at the foot of the mountains. It sat in the middle of a lovely yard surrounded by high walls that shielded them from curious eyes. She was secured in one of the most exclusive, private condominiums Santiago had to offer: Reina Alto.

CHAPTER 12

"The Calm Before the Storm"

"There is a silent justice that is accomplished inside each conscience."

EYES HALF-CLOSED, SARAH LET HER mind roam. She could hardly believe she had lived so many years in peace with her family in Reina Alto. Her children had grown up before her eyes before she had realized it!

The cheerful laughter of young women reached Sarah through her open car window. She had already been waiting for several minutes for Esther to join her after a birthday party at the home of one of her high school friends. This had been one of the few events her father allowed her to attend. It was hard for him to admit that his daughter was growing up and had become a tall, slim, striking sixteen-year-old. As she got into her mother's car her wavy dark hair bounced with her mood. Sarah smiled, admiring Esther's physical features that resembled those of her father. The sparkle of her light eyes, however, reflected the same brightness as her mother's.

Starting the car, they drove away, leaving the center of Santiago behind to head back to the neighborhood they had called home for the past ten years. On the way, they stopped at the Military School Sports Center to pick up John, who was waiting for them at the door. The three continued on their way as evening set in, the last rays of sun slipping away behind the nearby mountaintops.

The elegant vehicle entered the narrow driveway that led to the house. They passed through its iron gates, parked the car and blithely strolled into the house as Esther and John continued to chat about their afternoons. Sarah laughed, pretending to wish to escape their "intolerable babbling". Soon their voices muted and their laughter ceased. Hans' tall figure paced back and forth with long steps and a grave semblance.

Sarah turned on the lights to find her husband deeply burdened. Esther and John, sensing his strain, greeted him warmly before retiring to their rooms. Once they were alone, Sarah went to him and embraced him. Hans responded with a tender kiss on her cheek, and invited her to sit with him. She began to question him, "What's wrong, my love? Were you worried because we were late?"

"No, darling. It's something else. I was just informed that comrade Adolf Eichmann was executed in Ramla, Israel. They hung him. You remember he was kidnapped in Argentina by the Mossad agents. To think that the imprudence of his own children cost him his life today! And to die in such a terrible way...."

Sarah reacted violently, "Because his children had been too indulgent?! Have you forgotten how many thousands...no millions of people were executed after being tortured and raped? How many others served as rats for their experiments and...oh, the endless atrocities! And he was among those who gave the orders! I hope he was sorry for what he did!"

Hans stood up; her reply had made him uncomfortable. He turned his back towards her and carefully articulated, "You know that I have never agreed with the genocide and that I had no idea of what was going on until my plane crashed in Auschwitz and I saw it with my own eyes. Now this all has come into the light and the whole world is talking about it. Unfortunately, they are blaming the entire German nation, as if each citizen had been carrying these things out with our own hands."

Sarah interrupted, "But, he's dead now. What can you do about it?"

"Nothing for him. But this means a resurgence of hatred and, even worse, the need to mobilize everyone living as refugees in Argentina because we don't know who the Mossad will be after next."

"Do you think the agents could be in Chile now?" Sarah questioned nervously.

"They could be in any country, any province of South America."

"So, we're back to the persecutions and fear…our peace is over! What will happen to our children?" Sarah was confounded.

Hans tried to soothe her, "Calm down! Everything is under control. We just need to take precautions again like we have before."

"But our children are teenagers! What are we going to tell them this time? That we have to stay locked up in here without speaking to anyone?!"

"We'll just tell them not to talk to any strangers because there is a wave of kidnapping on the rise."

Sarah interrupted with irritation, "Oh great! How long do you think you can go on deceiving them?"

"I don't know," Hans said. "But I fear for your lives. They might be after me, too!"

Hans became more distressed as Sarah exploded, "I'm sick of the lies! Our entire marriage has been a lie!"

"What makes you say that?"

"Because I'm married to the name "Urik Mulet", the Swiss soldier who died in Portugal. Your children don't even carry your true last name! I don't know how much longer I can take this!" Sarah stormed out of the room, slamming the door behind her.

Klaus kept an old house outside of Santiago, on the way to Viña del Mar, as a refuge center for the Germans passing though Chile. Different leaders of ODESSA from Bolivia, Paraguay and Argentina met there for an emergency meeting. Hans left his home for several days to attend the meeting without explaining his whereabouts to Sarah, who was still disgusted with the whole situation. Part of Hans' obligation as administrator of the treasures in South America was to meet every so often with the *Kamaraden* to receive the latest updates from Europe and to obtain reports on the political situation of each continent.

There had been several changes of government since their last meeting, and they needed to discern how much protection the new governments would extend and how much that protection would cost them. However, the main reason they were meeting was to decide upon the sale of some invaluable works of art, some of which Hans had been keeping at this own residence: a Titian, Rembrandt's "Saskia

Sonriente", and a Corot. They could also agree upon the one of the many other works hidden away in the safes. Regardless, it was essential for them to have cash on hand for any movement of people deemed necessary, especially in light of the recent circumstances. The men at the meeting had agreed on the sale because Klaus had been able to hire a *marchand* who was willing to sell the works of art.

The week that Hans was gone, Sarah called David at his office in Buenos Aires, as was her weekly custom. Sarah immediately recognized the agreeable voice of the woman who answered the call: It was her sister-in-law Judith, whom she had met the past summer when David and she came to visit on their honeymoon. She was cousin to Carlos, David's friend with whom he went to study with in Buenos Aires. After greeting Sarah, Judith put David on the phone. He warmly greeted his sister, reminiscing about those happy days they had shared the summer before. Sarah chuckled with him at the memories before confiding that there was something that was worrying her. David's tone changed instantaneously and asked, "Now what's happening?"

An anguished Sarah faltered, "It's Hans."

"What about Hans?"

"He's afraid they're after him again."

"Oh, no! That nightmare again? It can't be!"

Sarah cried as she continued, "You know I don't fear from myself, but for my children. They are innocent! They had nothing to do with what happened! I've been thinking about what you told me long ago, that innocent or not, our children would one day suffer as a consequence of having covered up what those people have done. In return, we are lugging that curse with us forever."

Her sobs broke David's heart and he tried to calm her, but she was unrelenting, "I feel like I'm a prisoner again! A prisoner of an invisible jail from which I can't escape…!" Her voice faded away.

One the other line, the calm voice of David lulled, "You remember the 'Shepherd' I've told you about from Auschwitz? When I believed that I would never be free, he assured me, 'If the Son sets you free, you are free indeed!' Now I am convinced of who my true liberator is: JESUS, THE MESSIAH! Just trust him. The Eternal One will help you!"

His words were a balm to Sarah's anguished heart. Alleviated, Sarah agreed with David that she and her children had to leave

Santiago. They would make plans to leave for his house in Buenos Aires soon. As they said good-bye, he assured her that he loved her deeply and she could depend on him for help in any circumstance.

A month had passed since the meeting, and Hans had met with the *marchand* to deliver the Degas painting that was to be sold in Europe. In Milan the *marchand* would contact a member of ODESSA who would then inform Klaus of the negotiations. Klaus, in turn, would take the report to Hans, who would decide whether to accept the stipulated price or not.

As the days went on without word from the ODESSA contact in Milan, Klaus communicated with him to find out if he had met with the *marchand*. The contact said that the *marchand* had never arrived at his destiny. Immediately, Klaus commanded an investigation throughout Europe to see if the painting was on the market there.

From her room, Esther heard angry voices coming from her father's office. She snuck down the hall towards the office and put her ear up to the door to try to hear what was happening. She recognized her father's voice, but couldn't distinguish the irate voice of her "Uncle Klaus". She was unable to make out what they were fighting about. All of a sudden, Klaus' tone raised, "But Coronel Müller! How could I have known what would happen?"

Her father fumed, "Now we've lost that painting and, with it, thousands of dollars for the organization!"

The noise of steps approaching warned Esther that someone was coming down the hall. She quickly ran back to her bedroom, bumping into her mother on the stairs. Sarah had also heard the voices and was on her way to find out what was going on when the two collided. Noting the disturbance on her face, Sarah took her by the shoulders and led her to her room. Both sat on the bed. Esther impatiently asked Sarah about the reason for her father's anger. "What is going on? Why are they fighting?"

"I don't know, dear."

Esther's mind was full of questions that poured out of her lips, "Why did Uncle Klaus call dad 'Coronel Müller'? And why did dad call him 'Capitan Kramer'? What painting was lost? What organization?"

Sarah doesn't know where to start under the fire of her questions.

The young woman pressed, "Answer me, mother! I've noticed something strange happening for a long time now. I love father, but he's grown distant, as if he's afraid of my questions. And now this! I'm starting to feel I don't even know who my father is!"

Sarah's silence urged her even more, "Mother, why are you so quiet? Why won't you answer me?"

Sarah's mind was in chaos. How she longed to escape! But she couldn't leave her daughter in the uncertainty that was obviously hurting her.

Esther quieted and waited, her face still inquiring. Seeing there was no way out and tired of so many years of silence, Sarah's faint voice carefully disclosed the story of the troubles and suffering that had begun that night in Warsaw on October 11, 1940, the last Yom Kippur she spent with her family.

As the story progressed, the terrible scenes of what her mother and David went through during the war passed through her imagination... the death of her grandmother and her grandfather's disappearance! She could comprehend the grudge the Jewish people held against the Germans; they did not understand that not all of them were guilty of the genocide. *And after all that,* Esther considered, *mother has also tolerated the pain of having to keep all of this from us!*

"What I regret the most is that our futile attempts could not prevent all this useless misery!" Sarah sobbed.

Esther hugged her compassionately as they cried together.

After a few moments, the young woman broke the silence, asking her mother, "You do love father, don't you?"

"Very much so! I love you, too. Everything I've told you must remain a secret between you and me. I want you to promise me that you will never tell your father or your brother what I have shared with you today."

Esther, still hugging her mother, whispered in her ear, "I won't say anything."

Sarah, taking her from her arms and holding her hands, looked her directly in the eyes and said, "My sweet daughter, always remember this day. I will never forget it. Today I have finally allowed those rivers of suffering out of my heart. I only ask that if one day you consider breaking this promise, be sure that it will not do us any more harm."

CHAPTER 13

"Mortal Vortex"

"To weep is to spill small drops of the pain, sadness, or love that flow inside like a river."

THE NEXT FEW YEARS ADVANCED in relative tranquility for Hans and his family.

Esther became a journalist and worked as the Santiago correspondent for a daily newspaper based in Buenos Aires. She lived with her Uncle David and his family in the capital city, and her job allowed her to travel a great deal. She was even able to visit Israel, where she was able to visit many sights for a story she was doing for a seminary in Argentina.

When she returned, she told her mother how thrilled she was to visit the land of her ancestors and the indescribable sensation of the treading the Holy Lands, especially the Holy Tomb, where she deeply perceived the presence of God. Sarah was overjoyed at the fervent words of her daughter, and both agreed they would have to go together soon to fulfill Sarah's lifelong wish to visit the land of her forefathers.

Having her daughter in Buenos Aires allowed Sarah to travel frequently to Argentina. Esther had become independent and rented a stylish apartment in the middle of Barrio Norte where she received Sarah every time she visited. Sarah and David took advantage of those days as well, enjoying long walks and discussions which often lead to their persistent search for their father, Gabriel.

John, their youngest, had also finished his studies in engineering at the Santa Maria de Valparaiso University. When they visited, Hans and John got involved in long conversations. A deep love existed between them. The young man admired his father's integrity and recognized an unusual wisdom that could have only come from deep experiences that had marked his spirit. He knew he was capable of loving even when forced to make sacrifices. He had seen the deep pain that occasionally leaked through his father's silent, strong façade.

Many times he had wanted to know more about his father's uneasiness, but Hans had tightly sealed the door to any questions. John knew that he must love him as he was. They spent endless hours on the beach together, but what the young man enjoyed most were the hours flying with his father. Hans had taught John to fly a small plane, and both of them adored performing acrobats in the cloudless sky with the immeasurably majestic ocean at their feet.

At the demand of the ODESSA, Hans was obligated to sell more paintings and sculptures. He also had to mobilize more leaders that had returned from Europe, demanding the services of an acquaintance who was an oceanographer and investigator. The man was able to move through all the oceans of the world without raising any suspicions, being immune from investigation due to the recognition certain governments had endowed him. Thus, he could transport the paintings, sculptures and even men when necessary in the storage areas of his ships. His collaborations had smoothed over problems for the Nazi fugitives, many of whom had returned home with goods that allowed them to live comfortably when they arrived.

Hans had also procured a closer relationship with the government in Chile through the person of General Pinochet. They maintained a flowing friendship based on their shared ideals and views. Both held a great understanding of international geopolitics, and they would often get lost in long controversies surrounding those topics as they shared flights that Hans piloted as one of the president's personal aircraft aviators. Their relationship greatly benefited the organization's purposes, granting them the freedom to move about Chilean territory during the 1980s.

Sarah, uneasy with their closeness, kept her distance because she was secretly bothered by the impunity of those men who had done so much damage to humanity. The entire situation slowly deteriorated communication between Hans and Sarah. At times, she thought she would never recover those few short-lived days of happiness and peace they had lived with her husband in the south. She felt that, although she would always love him, their relationship had grown cold.

Hans, motivated by the similarities of thought between himself and Pinochet, got more involved in activities that kept him away from home. The meetings with Pinochet and his collaborators continued. They had been sent to La Paz, Bolivia to gather parts of the treasure that had been dispersed back in 1946 to lessen suspicions and for safer transport, because the ODESSA was demanding more cash. They had called a special meeting because the shipment was so important; they would unite their assets and send them to their organization stationed in the United States. The shipment would also allow them to establish new distribution bases because they would be able to integrate more capital into industries and commerce that would yield permanent earnings for the organization, moving money that was currently inactive. That capital together with the gold that had been sent throughout the 1970s represented a huge portion of the treasures of terror.

Hans returned home that night to dine with Sarah and John. Afterward dinner, they enjoyed a pleasant dessert. Everything appeared normal and untroubled, although the evening together was really spent in anticipation of John's upcoming departure. In just a few days he would be traveling to France to take a post-graduate course. The next morning they had to work out the last details of his trip, and because John's car was not working, Hans had offered his personal vehicle, which would be driven by his chauffeur. John didn't like the idea of using his father's car, but the urgency of the paperwork he needed to prepare compelled him to accept the offer with gratefulness.

Very early the next morning, while Sarah was still in bed, the men shared a brief breakfast before the young man headed to the center of the city. They said good-bye at the door and John got into the car, which slowly rolled towards the gate at the end of the driveway that joined their residence to the street. Just as the car reached the iron entrance, an explosion startled Hans. He ran to the window where he saw that the front end of the car had been almost completely destroyed; its pneumatics had burst open by the impact of the explosion. The driver fruitlessly tried to back the vehicle up, but they were stuck inside the immobile armor. Hans quickly grabbed his machine gun from a desk drawer and ran outside to the place where the entrance guard had already opened fire on the attacking commandos. Behind Hans, the guards who had been resting inside the house came running out.

Sarah was in her room, a prisoner of panic. She cried desperately, not daring to go out. She ran to her second-story window where she saw that the car was in the middle of open fire. She heard the angry voices of the men. Everything was happening so fast, even though Sarah felt as if she were moving in slow motion. Her son was trapped between the shots and worst of all, might already be wounded or dead. With a stiffening scream, the tense moment's hostage fainted.

Outside, the commandos began to flee when they saw that the surprise factor of their attack had failed. They were planning on assaulting the home but had been defeated by Hans' men. They continued to fight as they retreated, leaving a few wounded men behind. Hans approached the vehicle, from which his men were dragging a wounded man back to the house. In his despair, he impulsively opened the door John had unlatched from inside. The young man was pale and speechless; he fell into his father's arms, still trembling from the influence of what had just happened.

Father and son raced back to the house as some projectiles hit the surface of the car. Hans continued to fire his gun, covering their retreat.

Still dazed, Sarah came to and found herself lying on her bed. When she opened her eyes, she saw the dear faces of her husband and son. She desperately clung to John, crying, "My dear son! My son! What happened to you?"

The young man soothed her as she caressed his face, "Nothing, mom. Please, calm down."

Behind them, Sarah saw Hans' twitching face. She admonished him severely, "This was bound to happen some day! If something would have happened to our son, you would have been to blame!"

She cried bitterly, unleashing her agony, "I won't let you continue to hurt me! This is over! When John leaves for France, I'm going to Buenos Aires to live with Esther!"

Hans, powerless and aware that she was partially right, left the room without a word.

Before leaving for France, John tried to change his mother's mind and smooth over her conflict with his father. Sarah insisted that she needed some time away because the events of previous days had profoundly upset her.

When she arrived in Buenos Aires, Esther noticed an accentuated wince of sadness in her mother's countenance. On several occasions, she tried to get her to talk, but Sarah was pensive and quiet. At night, Esther believed she heard smothered cries coming from her mother's bedroom. She was determined to find out why she was so sad, so she planned a long walk through a nearby park to distract her and compel her to open her heart.

The sunny, September afternoon beckoned them to enjoy the sun's warm rays. Mother and daughter walked through a narrow path in the park, watching the cheery children and young people. There, in the atmosphere of recreation, Esther warmly embraced her mother and whispered in her ear, "I love you, mom!"

"I love you, too, daughter," Sarah replied. "I love you all so much. How I love my family!"

"I know, mom. That is why I am so concerned; I see you are not happy. What unsettles you so? John is studying, I'm happy with my job, and you and dad are finally alone and can spend more time together."

Sarah interrupted, "This is precisely about your father and me. You know our story. You know how deeply we have loved, but you also know about the enormous burden we have carried in our consciences: I, for having concealed as much as I know to the harm of my own people and family; your father, for the obligation he believed was an act of loyalty to his country, and even now as he is growing old, that loyalty costs him our happiness." As the tears weld up in her eyes, she concluded, "I'm more convinced each day that the weight of this guilt will end up wearing us down completely, destroying our love."

Esther, who had been silently listening to her mother, intervened, "But mom, it can't be! When will this persecution...this sensation of oppression that doesn't let us experience true freedom end? We are constantly enslaved to some fear or uncertainty. Just because I have

Jewish roots, I have been discriminated on several occasions. What would happen if people knew that my father is a German of the Nazi regime?"

"Now you understand why I feel this way, devoid of the courage and strength I need to continue. Now, with the attack on your brother, I have seen the violence break out around us again and I have felt like we have returned to the past to repay the interminable debt of pain that your father and those he protects have to the world. I feel that, in our lives, the deaths and the torture we believed we had escaped when we left Europe have been repeated again and again no matter where we have fled. Every once in a while, God uses those men that hound us to remind us that the debt has not been paid yet."

Esther observed her mother, surprised at her words. "How do you think this debt can be paid? What would be the price?"

Sarah answered, "It's impossible. Only the sincere repentance of all those men would have extenuated the hatred and resentment, but now many of them have died without expressing the most minimal remorse."

"But father?" Esther asked anxiously, "Has he repented? What do you think, mother?"

"Yes, I believe so. He's often expressed his remorse for having continued in all of this."

Frustrated Esther interrupted, "Then why doesn't he just renounce it already?"

"That would never have been easy. Remember that all the weight of administrating and safeguarding those chests is on him. And what truly tortures me now is thinking that those men have found your father and may attack us again."

"Don't think that! Don't even say it!"

The conversation with her mother, instead of calming Esther, disquieted her even more. She loved her parents, but she couldn't intervene to help them because she had made a covenant of silence with her mother that impeded speaking openly with her father.

The days went by slowly for Hans; he was waiting for Sarah's return. Surrounded by guards, he felt more isolated each day. The nightmares had returned. At times he felt besieged, persecuted; he painfully recognized that lately he had shared very little time with his family. He loved them so much. He knew he had never meant to harm them, especially his beloved Sarah. How many times had he regretted obeying the orders of his superiors when everything was in chaos! He should have never taken that cursed plunder out of Europe. Sarah and David were right! The gold stolen from the Jews had never made any of them happy.

The days seemed interminable. In his loneliness, he wanted to run and beg his family's forgiveness for his cowardice, for not renouncing it all. It would have been difficult though not impossible to start a new life anywhere in the world without the weight of so many deaths on their shoulders. As night approached, he tried to sleep, but it was impossible. At times he hallucinated, imagining the suffering faces of tortured, mutilated bodies mixed with scenes of his airplane falling among the trees surrounding Auschwitz.

He woke up and the clock showed that it wasn't even ten o'clock. How he needed the caresses and warm voice of his Sarah! The house was dead quiet. Anguished, he went out to get some fresh air, walking towards a small park close to the house. Even the streetlights could not disperse the dense, heavy darkness that surrounded him, although Hans barely seemed to notice.

He knew that he could walk freely here, but he still kept his hand on the gun in his coat pocket. Before he knew it, he had arrived at the park's security fence. He did not observe any strange movements around him, but something unusual surprised him in the guard house: the entrance was dark. He instinctively began to retreat, trying to retrace his steps.

Shadowy figures slowly appeared in the darkness, followed by the buzz of bullets shot with a silencer. He felt the sting of the impacts and quickly tried to pull the weapon out of his pocket, but a bright flash wounded him and a muffled death rattle accompanied the falling of his body. Behind him, his men began to unleash a counter attack against the enemies. Hans got up and tried to evade the line of fire, but his legs would not respond. He laid there, blood spilling from numerous wounds on his body.

The gunfire continued for a few more brief moments until the intruders fled, leaving behind various corpses as proof of the damage inflicted by the shots. In the distance, they heard a vehicle speeding away. Hans felt very weak. He tried to speak to his men, but his vision became cloudy...

CHAPTER 14

"Yom Kippur"
(The Sun of Righteousness)

"The people who walked in darkness saw a great light."
Isaiah 9:1-7

ALTHOUGH IT HAD BEEN MANY years since Hans' disappearance, Sarah had not completely recovered from her loss. The memory of her beloved husband was forever present in her thoughts. The birth of her grandchildren was the only thing that managed to ease her pain. She kept remembering the events that occurred since that terrible night when Dietrich called to tell her that Hans and Klaus had been attacked at their residence. The affair was silenced, so that there would be no mention of it in the press, and they were warned not to discuss the incident publicly. When the sorrowful, blunt announcement was made, Esther had to support Sarah to keep her faint body from falling to the floor.

What happened afterwards was still foggy in her head. She only remembered that she had traveled home with David and Esther. When they entered their old residence, it felt strange and cold. The house that had been their home for decades suddenly had no life. Alone and empty, its silent rooms echoed many distant memories for Sarah and her family. Sarah realized that without Hans, everything had lost its color, as if life itself had fled. She barely remembered the conversation she had with Capitan Dietrich when she arrived in Chile; just a few questions had remained engraved in her mind.

The only thing that was clear was that her beloved Hans had been attacked, along with Klaus. Dietrich explained that when he arrived, he did not find either of their bodies, just some traces of blood, which had already been cleaned up and some empty shells: inconclusive evidence. The only thing that was certain is that they were missing. David and Dietrich went to work with some of their contacts in the government to search for them, but it was useless: No one knew anything. After several days of futile efforts, they halted the search.

Esther and David had to return to their respective obligations, but Sarah decided to stay a little longer. She held a secret hope of Hans' return. She received calls daily, urging her to return to Buenos Aires and to close up the house. After a long month, she decided to return to Buenos Aires with Esther.

The evening before her trip, she was very disturbed by the thought of abandoning her home without any news or sign from Hans. The house seemed lonelier and emptier than ever. Sarah went to her room early. Her housemaid brought her some warm milk, affectionately telling her to drink it while it was still warm to help her fall asleep. Despite her recommendations, Sarah stayed awake for a long while.

The hours went by and the grandfather clock showed that it was after four o'clock in the morning. Sarah suddenly heard a soft sound that interrupted the silence that surrounded the house. She paid close attention to the stealth steps that approached through the garden. She jumped out of bed, her heart racing. She was somewhat afraid, but a fluttering of hope gave her courage.

She cautiously moved towards the living room just as something brushed against the front door. She stopped, petrified in the tense expectation of the door opening to reveal the strange night visitor. However, after a few moments, the anxiety ceased as she heard the steps move away. She dashed to the window just in time to see Captain Klaus' well-known figure disappearing into the shadows.

Still trembling, she turned on the lights and was surprised to see an envelope that had been slipped under the door. She took it in her hands, turned the lights off again and went back to the intimacy of her room, where she ripped the envelope open anxiously longing to see what was inside. Several papers fell out. She took the first of them, which was a letter in which Klaus briefly explained that the rest of the envelope's contents were papers Hans had ordered him to keep; they were only to be delivered to Sarah if something happened to Hans. Klaus' brief letter ended with an insistent request for Sarah to keep silent about the envelope's contents as well as the identity of the messenger, especially in front of Dietrich.

Curious, she began to read the rest of the contents, recognizing immediately the unmistakable penmanship of Hans. Emotion overwhelmed her; tears blurred her vision. The letters danced before her eyes. She finally held, in her hands, something that could indicate her husband's destiny! Among the papers, a small envelope caught her eye, magnetically drawing her. Between muffled sobs, she devoured its words:

> My very beloved Sarah,
>
> I had always hoped we would to grow old together, but instability has always surrounded our existence, although it has never affected our love, which will remain in my heart in spite of any separation or distance. Know that you will always live in my heart beyond death itself.
>
> I confess myself guilty of not loving you more, of not knowing how to show my love enough lately. The same goes for my dear children: Esther and John.
>
> I write these lines with the thought that in your absence something could happen to me. You know everything is uncertain for me.
>
> I want you to know that I have never loved anyone as I have loved you. I am not angry with you, and I have often regretted not having abandoned this mission in Portugal. I know that we would have been very happy and nothing could have ever separated us. Do you remember the song you taught me when we were walking along the lake? The one your mother taught you from the Torah:
>
> > "Place me like a seal over your heart;
> > Like a seal on your arm;
> > For love is as strong on death."

> My treasure, whenever you remember me, love me as I am! I have given Klaus orders to deliver these envelopes to you if anything happens to me. They contain instructions about what to do if I am gone.
>
> Kisses from your beloved husband,
>
> Hans

Crying distraughtly she continued to review the rest of the papers in the envelope. Among them were the titles to the ranch in Osorno and the house in Bariloche along with an inventory of the valuable objects found at both properties. Still in awe, she read the final instructions that were attached. Hans had placed everything in Sarah's name, which allowed her access to a small fortune...well, a fortune that was not so small because, selling all assets, it would amount to several million dollars.

She would be able to keep a small part of the money. Another portion, in accordance with Hans' will, would be given to charity. Hans' special wish was to establish a children's home for orphans. However, the majority of the funds would be given to the German government for the collections being taken to pay indemnifications to the descendants of the Jewish people. The last paragraph of the document danced before her: Its message hit her deep inside, as if she could hear Hans' beloved voice pronouncing the message written there:

> My beloved Sarah,
>
> I know that money could never rectify your people's physical and psychological suffering, but at least it is more tangible than a simple verbal recognition.
>
> I want you to know that this is my way of making amends, in part, for my personal guilt in having helped to take away the plunder. I've repented many times, and I hope that this action will free you and our children from the burden of pain and remorse that you should have never carried. My beloved Sarah, it would be so beautiful for this compensation to stand

as a symbol of forgiveness between our nations, and
as a good message for the rest of the world....

A knocking on the door of her bedroom in Buenos Aires made Sarah jump, tears still in her eyes. Esther's voice brought her back to the present. Once again, without realizing it, she had gotten lost in her memories as her mind returned to the moment Hans had disappeared the year before. Esther persisted in knocking at the door. Recomposing herself, Sarah opened the door to allow her daughter in. Concerned by her delay in opening, Esther hugged and kissed her affectionately before asking, "What's wrong, mom? Were you remembering again?"

"Not intentionally, darling. What happened is not easy to forget."

"I know, mom. But what you are doing for those children is so wonderful. The home you have organized is such an amazing place. Aren't you satisfied to see so many happy children around you? Besides, look at the headlines of today's newspaper. Father would be so happy! The indemnification payments to the Jewish descendants of the Holocaust victims are going into effect. Doesn't this please you?"

"Yes, very much. We have been carrying out your father's will, and he would be thrilled."

"I believe, mother, that it means much more than that. Finally, we have been freed from that curse: you, us, our children..." With an air of cunning she tilted her head, allowing her long black locks to fall onto her cheek, "...and someday, you will let me tell the story."

Sarah frowned at her, "You know what you promised me,"

Esther, moving towards the door, cheerfully reminded her, "Hurry, mom. Did you forget that they are expecting us at Uncle David's?"

In Esther's car, on the way to her brother's home, Sarah and her daughter talked about the birthday preparations for her granddaughter, Ruth.

Sarah had been very surprised that the entire family had been filmed and by the questions of the young reporter, who according to Esther was Ruth's boyfriend.

"Do you know what was so strange to me, dear? The celebration is for my granddaughter, yet they were asking me about my life. They even asked about my father. Oh Father! What must have been become of my beloved father? David never ceases to look for him, but to no avail. It would be a miracle if we were to find something about father after so long."

"My uncle says that he will never stop searching, as long as he lives because they made a covenant."

The conversation continued until they arrived at David's house. When they entered the living room, everything was very bright. There the young man was again with his camera and his friend who helped with the microphone. Everyone was happy at this an intimate celebration. The only guests were Sarah and David with his wife, and both of their respective children and grandchildren. They had been planning on getting everyone together like this for a long time. David hugged Sarah and, taking her by the shoulders, invited her to sit on the living room sofa.

It was a cold August night. The frigid air beat against the windows, frosting it with crystals. The warmth inside the home where the entire family gathered together contrasted with the cold, fierce weather outside. Everyone was cheerful, joking and laughing. Soon, the young reporter, who had been silently filming them, asked everyone for their attention. As everyone looked at him, Ruth smiled mischievously. The young man spoke, "Quiet, please. Your attention, please. Ruth has something to tell you."

Everyone hushed, and a bit excitedly the young woman looked towards Sarah and David, pausing as if she wanted to create suspense before continuing, "Grandfather David, you know why I wanted to celebrate my birthday at your house and with all of our family together, especially with you, Aunt Sarah," she said, her voice breaking with emotion. "I know that when it's someone's birthday, people give gifts to honor that person, but this year I want to give you a surprise present for which you have been waiting a long time. Let's turn off the lights!"

Everyone began to murmur, assuming it would be the movie her boyfriend had been working on for the last few days.

"Quiet please!" Ruth insisted. "I want you to close your eyes until I tell you to open them. It will be like the game we played when we were children and grandfather wanted to surprise us. Remember grandfather? Remember Aunt Sarah? Right? Okay...now! You can open your eyes! Surprise!!!"

An elderly, thin, bald man smiled radiantly as he moved towards the living room, just steps away from David and Sarah. The silence was absolute; no one even ventured a breath.

A muffled cry escaped David's lips as he arose from his seat to hug his father.

"Father!" Sarah exclaimed.

The three embraced in an endless, wordless hug until the emotion and tension of the moment were broken by the applause and whistles of the rest of the family.

The young man with the camera then explained that he was not Ruth's boyfriend. He was a reporter from a television program that helped people find their lost families and that Ruth had written to share the story of Gabriel, David and Sarah. With much effort, they had found Gabriel living in Israel, still hoping to find his children and wife.

The surprise was so tremendous that it took quite a while to recover.

That weekend they were invited to another program, once again finding themselves being interviewed before the camera. Everything happened so fast, as if the three were in a dream. The questions were quick and direct.

"You are happy, aren't you?" the reporter began. "How long had you been separated and why?"

With tears, David fearlessly answered, "We had received no news of father since 1944." He smiled and patted him. "The last time we had seen him was in Auschwitz, in the Second World War."

"Are you Jews?"

"Yes," Sarah replied.

"What do you remember about what you experienced?" Looking at Gabriel, the interviewer added, "I imagine you have a lot to tell."

With a slow, broken voice the elderly man answered, "Maybe what I am going to tell you is not what you are expecting, but I believe that it is not time to remember, but rather time to forget. Too much has already been said and the more we talk, the more resentment grows. It is time to allow the Most High to judge men, not us."

Surprised by his answer, the young man smiled at the camera and continued, "What will you do now that you are together again?"

David replied, "We will spend time in family to make up for lost time after so many years of separation. We have so much to tell each other!"

"Yom Kippur is just a few days away, right? What will you do?"

"We will celebrate in Jerusalem. We are going to spend the holiday with father, celebrating as we did fifty years ago. When we light the candles we will remember our mother, Ruth, and our brother, Elijah."

"What does Yom Kippur signify for you?" the young man inquired.

"It is a time of atonement and forgiveness when we ask the Eternal God to forgive us for our offenses to others and when we forgive the offenses of those who have harmed us. This year it will not only be for our own family but for all of the families that were victims of the Holocaust. We must pray, asking Adonai to help us forgive even our enemies. That is what this very important day of Yom Kippur is about," Sarah explained.

"How beautiful!" the reporter commented.

"And how good it would be," reflected Gabriel, broken by emotion, "for the whole world to see the day when men decide to forgive and ask forgiveness. How many wars…how much pain…how much damage humanity would avoid! The eternal one has not forgotten his children; finally the pain, the curse and the bitterness end for my family and my Jewish people!"

The camera passed slowly over the faces of David, Sarah, Esther, John, Ruth, and their families; each face tearful yet smiling hope. The reporter, also impressed by the scene and unable to dissimulate his emotion, ended the interview.

Meanwhile, in a remote village of South America, another aging man warmed himself by the fireplace. Filled with emotion for what he had just seen on the television screen, he sat beside his friend, Klaus, who painfully watched him. Both were staggered by what they had seen.

Tears flooded Hans' face. Right there in front of them, they saw Sarah, David, John, Esther and their children. They couldn't believe it! The camera continued moving from face to face, tearing Hans' heart out. There was his beloved family! He didn't exactly understand what was going on, but he felt that something had also been released inside of him. A deep sigh escaped his lips, and it was as if so many years of carrying the weight of guilt left with it. The tears that seemed to flow from his eyes were really coming from his heart. At last, he was truly FREE! Even without his family at his side, he accepted that his renouncement had been the fair price he had to pay.

The days following the encounter with their father were the happiest Sarah and David had lived since that last evening in Warsaw. They had decided to unite at Gabriel's house in Jerusalem, the land of their forefathers where Gabriel had decided to reside. Together they enjoyed the Holy Land and all the sacred memories it held; their eyes delighted in seeing the places they had read about their whole lives. For Sarah, it was the fulfillment of a deep yearning, something she had always desired even before knowing her father was there.

Time passed quickly for them. They were rejoicing in the pleasure of simply being together in their father's house after so many years of bitter separation. As the Yom Kippur celebration drew to an end, announcing the conclusion of the fast and time of atonement, they joyfully felt in their spirits that the Eternal One had forgiven their failures, that they were liberated from resentment and suffering. They had forgiven and had asked for forgiveness, opening the doors for the peace of the Most High to reign in their hearts!

In the midst of the uncontainable gladness, Gabriel, Sarah and David embraced tightly. They had finally recovered the image of that special day together as a family. Now they could celebrate, thanking the Eternal One for what they had longed for so often: "The Day of Atonement".

Suddenly, the doorbell rang, echoing in the imposed silence that was tradition for the closing of the ceremony. The housemaid entered the dining room with a package that she silently placed in Gabriel's hands. Surprised, he opened the wrapping. As the paper fell, a polished, shiny candlestick appeared to explode with incredible brilliance. Gabriel placed it upon the table. Drawn to it, everyone moved closer without speaking. Something strange was happening. A special light flooded the room; everyone was stirred, feeling the very presence of the Most High.

Sarah wondered what that candlestick was doing there. It seemed she had seen it someone before. Gabriel had already identified it, taking it into his hands again and examining it with a strange premonition. Confirming his suspicion, his eyes discovered the names he had carved on it fifty years ago in Warsaw. His sight blurred with tears as he imagined the dear figure of his wife lighting the candles as part of that celebration they shared together.

The candlestick had caught Sarah's attention, too. A small, handwritten card hung from one of the arms. A chill ran up her spine. She recognized that penmanship! The message went straight to her heart; a single one word danced before her eyes: FORGIVENESS!"

Suddenly Sarah broke the quietness of the moment, running to open the door. She saw a man in the distance and moved towards him slowly, leaving Gabriel speechless behind her. Without even blinking her eyes, worn by age and so many tears, she watched the man who stood under the shadows. A wild, merry ringing in her chest drowned her breathing. It couldn't be! It had to be an optical illusion. The man standing on the corner of the street appeared to be....No! No! It couldn't be! One last ray of light in the twilight reflected the aging figure of her beloved. After a few moments of hesitation, she hastened towards him, a prayer flowering on her lips:

"Place me like a seal over your heart,
Like a seal on your arm;
For love is as strong as death."

In an instant, an embrace like the ones that had united them before connected them once again in an interminable caress that enveloped the love they contained in their hearts.

Gabriel moved forward with slow, unsteady steps to meet them under the clearness of the sky illuminated by myriad hues of the sunset.

Hearing him, Hans pulled Sarah from his arms. The men looked at each other, a warm light caressing their faces. Gabriel moved closer. Sarah silently extended her hand to take her father's. Hans extended his. For just a moment, their eyes shined strangely before their hands joined. Sarah hugged them both and held their hands together as a supernatural light penetrated them, melted them, and sealed them.

The father's voice was deep, "Welcome home, children!"

From the expectant silence of the streets the blast of the shofar sounded far off. It was the Eternal One's most beautiful response, declaring FORGIVENESS AND FREEDOM! Songs broke out the streets, surrounding them in peace and the presence of the Most High. "Peace be with you...."

"Shalom Aleichem
Mal'achei hasharet
Mal'achei elyon
Mimelech mal'achei ham'lachim
Hakadosh baruch Hu...."

EPILOGUE

Esther Asser Mulet's teary eyes stung as they readjusted to the movie theater's serene lights, which had just flicked on, marking the end of the debut of the film based on her novel.

From somewhere in the tangible hush, an explosion of thunderous applause broke out, flooding every last corner of the theater. The people around her began to greet her and congratulate her, embracing her with the emotion the film had aroused. Reporters rushed to her and bombarded her with questions before she had time to compose herself.

"Did you ever dream you would meet with such success?" was the first question a television reporter threw at her.

Esther, still stirred by the reaction of the viewers attending the opening night of the movie answered, "No, I mean...I never thought...I never imagined this kind of response."

"What inspired the plot of your story?" another reporter asked.

"My family's suffering, my own life!" she briefly replied.

"What do you mean your own life?" asked another young man.

"My own experiences. Much of the story is real. I am the daughter of the main characters."

A dense murmuring followed her declaration.

"What made you decide to share this story after so long?"

"The belief that the truth must be told, even if it is delayed, especially in unresolved situations like this one."

"Why unresolved?"

"Simply put, because even though so much time has gone by, the resentment and hatred between the nations involved lingers. People were very hurt, but it is unfair for the children to have to pay for the errors their parents made so many years ago, don't you think? That is why it is still a current topic."

"Do you consent for the crimes to go unpunished?" chimed another reporter.

"I believe that each and every one of the responsible parties has already been judged, maybe not by man but by life itself and by God, who never allows the unrepentant guilty to go free. Even the grandchildren of those men still carry the curse, but I believe that it is time to break that bondage.

"I would like to tell those people that they are innocent; that the descendants of those destructive men do not have to carry their burden of guilt because that is not fair. The grandchildren and great-grandchildren weren't there; most of them had not even been born. It's time for them to stop bearing the stigma of the terrible mistake of their ancestors."

"And how can something like that occur," someone else asked, "while the differences among Jews and Germans continue?"

"It can only happen when we forget resentment and leave what was lived behind as a sad lesson of something that must never happen again. It would be good for the countries involved to get together to write the "blank book" that was not written half a century ago—a page that erases the ones that were written with blood in the darkest night of our history. Then our children can learn from our forgiveness and forgetfulness."

As Esther made her declaration, a delicate, elderly woman approached her, accompanied by a handsome elderly man who was smiling from ear to ear. Sarah and David had finally been able to make their way through the circle of reporters surrounding Esther. Her rosy, tearful cheeks exposed the overflow of an internal culmination of emotions.

When Esther saw them, she quieted. An embrace was inevitable. They squeezed each other tightly as the tears ran freely down their cheeks. The writer tried to smile at the representatives of the press, who were watching in respectful silence.

"Forgive me. I have nothing more to say except to tell you that writing the truth of that story has finally brought healing to the wounds of the past, the wounds of my family."

The three slowly began to walk away together, Sarah between them. As they departed, in an imperceptible whisper she thanked the Eternal One that today, the truth had set them completely FREE! In Sarah's mind, Hans was as spotless and radiant as ever as his smiling lips proclaimed, "We are finally FREE!"

United by the same thought, Esther's voice rang in her ear, "You must have loved father very much, didn't you?"

Sarah looked into her eyes and spoke from the bottom of her heart, "Yes, I have always loved him. I still love him. Our love is so real that it will live on inside of us forever, like a burning flame that cannot be snuffed out!

"At last, today we can experience the only true freedom: the freedom of the Spirit. We have asked for forgiveness and the Eternal One has taught us to forgive. It will take some time, but there will be reconciliation in many hearts. This year, we will live the true YOM KIPPUR!"

"If hatred, violence and rancor have locked your heart in their prison, the only key that will open the door and set you free is....forgiveness."
SILVIA RUARTE FUNES